FOR WHICH WE STAND

Luke Kent

1.

The sun was just beginning to fall behind the buildings, dropping the temperature and providing a welcome respite from the scorching heat of the day. Dusk was always cooler in Texas. Ray Tucker walked quickly toward the parking garage on Colorado Street, uphill on 9th Avenue from Congress Avenue. He weaved into the maze of construction barricade shelters that were a perpetual fixture in Austin's downtown area. The scent of human urine was strong, magnified by the earlier heat of the day and the enclosure of the barricades.

A homeless man in tattered sweat pants and part of a t-shirt lay in front of the door to the parking garage when he arrived. Ray met eyes with him and before he could ask him to move the man asked "You got a dollar?"

"No, sorry buddy, I don't. Can I get by you here?" Ray never went out of his way to be rude to the homeless, despite their incessant requests for money as throngs of them descended upon the downtown workforce daily. He didn't even ignore them as most people did. He just politely told them he had no money to give them and went about his business.

The man rolled to the side, just enough to clear the door from hitting him, and Ray stepped over him and into the garage. The elevator ride to the fourth level was stifling, there was no air conditioning and the elevator car efficiently trapped the heat of the day. Ray looked at his cellphone for the time. It was just past eight o'clock, at least traffic would be light at this time. As he got into his Toyota Highlander and started it up, he thought about the homeless man at the entrance. He couldn't quite decide how he felt about him. He didn't pity him really, nor did he dislike him. He considered it odd that a man could ask a stranger for money without any remorse, explanation, or any emotion at all. Ray's denial of the request had been met with an equal lack of emotion by the man.

Ray concluded that his own feelings were much like those of the man who had asked him for the money, basically numb. He was not a fool and he completely understood that his dollar would have done absolutely nothing to help the man. If it would, he would have happily given it. Nonetheless, this homeless man and others like him represented no small portion of the political animus playing out at City Hall right now.

Pulling out of the garage and onto the road, Ray was thankful that the rush hour traffic had faded. The hour-long drive home was exponentially longer during the Austin rush hour. The City had not kept up with the population explosion in terms of infrastructure and as a consequence its roads were easily overwhelmed by the daily commute of people to and from the City. Traffic in the downtown area was so congested that emergency vehicles had difficulty responding to calls during certain periods of the day.

The highway was soothing as Ray pushed up against the 75 mile per hour speed limit, and he was glad to be leaving the City. There was a tension in the air that was palpable, and it dissipated as he gained distance from it. He played the meeting he had just watched over in his head as he drove, wondering how all of this was going to play out.

Austin's City Board were a mix of liberals and progressives. There were no moderates left, and the last conservative to hold a seat on the board decided not to run for a second term after numerous credible threats of sexual assault and death were made against her and her family. There was no longer any voice of opposition on the board, and even public testimony was met with heckling and threats if a conservative viewpoint were expressed. The re-election of the current President seemed to move the city even further left, and the rise of the Resistance was prominent in Austin generally, but on the University of Texas in particular. The Resistance lived up to its name. It had no specific issues to pursue other than to resist anything that might be seen as politically conservative.

Ray was a policy analyst for the Liberty Policy Foundation, a conservative think tank, and was no stranger to testifying before the state legislature or Austin's City Board. Recently, the Foundation had taken the rare position of no longer offering public testimonies out of concerns for safety. Policy analysts would now simply monitor the meetings for information to be put to use in position papers or for legal action through the Foundation's attorneys, but individual testimony had become too risky. There was no one on the Board interested in listening to a conservative or free market idea anyway, so it would have been mostly a wasted effort.

Fights were not uncommon at the board meetings, mostly between progressives and liberals who could not agree on what was "too far" or "not far enough." Most of the other conservative groups based in the area had stopped appearing at the meetings at all. Ray considered that they very well could be there in the same undercover capacity as he was attending them in, but felt sure he would recognize them if they did.

There were no Austin police officers at the meetings, they had been banned by the City Board from appearing anywhere public testimony would occur due to pressure from several of the anti-police groups in the area. The presence of police officers was considered oppressive to minorities. That no one had been shot yet was a miracle, perhaps due mostly to the left's general disdain for firearms. At any meeting, roughly a third of the public attending were wearing masks or hoods to hide their faces. Black hoodies, with or without the anarchy symbol, were the preferred mode of dress for many in attendance.

Ray had been among them this evening. A long sleeve gray t-shirt hid the coiled snake and "Don't Tread On Me" lettering tattooed on his forearm. The Gadsden flag tattoo would have marked him as a conservative and he would have needed to fight his way out. A black balaclava concealed his face, blending him in with the crowd. He took some satisfaction in the irony that the very same balaclava that made this group of crazies think he was one of them was the same one he had worn on too many SWAT raids to count. *If only they knew.*

Tonight's meeting had been particularly disturbing. Austin's City Board members voted unanimously not to allow the state legislature to meet in "their" city anymore. The mayor read aloud a statement that was meant to sound like the Declaration of Independence, including their list of grievances against the state government. Among these were the State Legislature's "insistence on overturning the City's lawfully enacted ordinances through state statutes." Specifics included the state mandate to cooperate with ICE officials on immigration issues, the passage of the "bathroom bill" that required a person to use the restroom assigned to their biological sex, and the overturning of a City tax on homes over $500,000 with a 22% property tax to fund homeless communes. All of these issues had been voted in as city ordinances passed by Austin, and all were almost immediately invalidated through Attorney General initiated lawsuits or bills passed by the state's overwhelmingly conservative legislature and signed by the governor prohibiting them. Austin's progressive activist ordinances had succeeded in making the state of Texas more conservative than ever, effectively outlawing the passage of similar ordinances anywhere in the state. The ideology of Austin was more and more in stark contrast with the rest of the state. Even the larger cities like Houston and Dallas, Democrat strongholds for years, were not approaching anywhere near the progressive activism that Austin was driving forth.

The reading of this declaration concluded with the City of Austin proclaiming its sovereignty and attached all ordinances that had been made unlawful by state action through the courts or legislature in the past five years as fully in effect immediately. The last sentence drew Ray's attention: "There will be no quarter for bigots or Nazis in Austin, and the State's elected officials and their conservative views represent outlawed hate speech and shall be henceforth banned from convening within City limits or from speaking publically in same." Austin was declaring sovereignty, seceding from the State of Texas, and disregarding the Constitution of the United States.

Upon passage, the Austin Chief of Police entered the room. Chief Wilshire had made national news as the recently appointed transgender woman was the first to lead a big city police department. She had not been a police officer upon appointment, but was instead a LGTBQ rights activist and friend of the mayor. Her passage through the Austin Police Academy was suspect, and the staff at the academy resigned just prior to her graduation from the academy and official appointment as chief, claiming they would not be a part of the sham that her graduation would represent. Austin's progressive community dismissed the resignations as the welcome purge of bigots and racists from the city's police department. Chief Wilshire now walked awkwardly in high heel shoes and her police uniform, smiling broadly while waving a sheet of paper as she approached the microphone. There was nothing feminine about her, and at six feet two inches tall she towered over those around her in her heels.

"I have here in my hand a signed warrant for the arrest of Governor Leland for trespassing on City property in his mansion," she said to raucous applause from the crowd. "Our City Magistrate has signed this, authorizing the arrest of the Governor if he does not vacate the residence in 48 hours." The timing coincided with the beginning of the Legislative Session in two days, also apparently banned.

It was at this point that Ray had left the meeting. Driving home out in the country made the whole event seem like he had just watched a movie at the theater. Not a good movie either, one where the plot is fun but so implausible that every part of it seems too much to be relatable. There was no indication of the craziness that was Austin out here in Salado. Ray pulled onto the gravel drive and looked at the small house on the large lot that he called his own. He put the car in park and rubbed his temples for a moment to collect his thoughts. *"What the hell had happened"*, he thought aloud. More importantly, *"what the hell is about to happen?"*

2.

Governor Tim Leland sat at the head of a round mahogany table. Seated around him were the Attorney General, the Lieutenant Governor, the Superintendent of the Texas Department of Public Safety, and a host of staffers. Tim Leland was an imposing figure. A former DPS trooper, he was a no nonsense kind of person. He wore an impeccable suit accented by his black ostrich boots. A Colt 1911 with authentic ivory grips rode in a custom leather holster on his hip, concealed by his coat.

"I am trying to keep a rational head about me on this, this, this….bullshit!" he began, slamming his fist on the table. "Who the hell do they think they are, these fuckin' hippies?" He continued, his rage barely contained.

Grace Headey had been the Attorney General for five years, three of them under this governor. She was a slim, intelligent woman. Her beauty and her conservative beliefs made her a constant target of attack by leftist commentators who felt she was a traitor to her sex. She was not intimidated, never had been, and she showed that now.

"Sir, I know I don't need to tell you this, but they have no lawful authority to…"

"Jesus, Grace, I know they don't!" Tim interrupted her but not in a condescending way. They were good friends, and she was not offended.

"I know, I had to say it though," she conceded.

"If those wacko cops they got working in this city show up at my door thinking they are going to arrest me, there's going to be a damn shootout, that much I know," Tim seethed.

The Superintendent of DPS was a longtime friend of Tim's, both had worked in patrol together. Jack Donaldson was a skilled, professional police officer and no one to trifle with. He had fourteen professional MMA fights under his belt before retiring from the sport at the urging of Tim, who had been reluctant to appoint him as head of DPS while he was still fighting professionally due to the bad optics. He spoke with a slow, Texas accent, in direct contrast to the explosive ability of his body. Despite his fighting background, Jack was prudent and cautious.

"Tim, my guy inside that meeting just informed me that two thirds of Austin PD just up and quit. No one there has more than three years on the job now. They just lost 800 officers," he said, looking at the text on his cellphone.

Three years ago, the Austin Police Department was forced by the City Board members to change its hiring practices and brought an influx of leftist activists to the agency. Morale at the agency had been in a downward spiral ever since, and the appointment of Chief Wilshire had been the final nail in the coffin. Word had spread through the department of tonight's intended actions, and everyone hired prior to the changes in hiring, everyone, had their resignation in hand should it happen. All 804 officers emailed the chief simultaneously, resigning effective immediately. The entire Austin Police Department was now in the hands of the transsexual chief and her crew of progressive activist officers. The four hundred remaining officers were a smattering of leftist activist groups, many of them from out of state, primarily California.

"Great, now the *only* ones left are the wackos," Tim shook his head. "Mark my word, I have no issue with killing them if they show up."

"I have the State SWAT team headed here now, and three dozen troopers set for crowd control around the perimeter," Jack said. "No one is getting in, Tim."

Grace looked at Jack and said, "I am researching criminal charges against the chief and the City Board as we speak. I am concerned, however, with the conflict that could be brewing when either side tries to enforce these warrants."

"I'm not," Tim said defiantly. "See that flag?" Tim pointed to a flag on the wall with a cannon and a five point star. "It says 'Come and Take It.' That is my response to them. And if we decide criminal charges are appropriate against *them*, I will bring the whole state of Texas down on their heads to enforce it. The Legislature had better dissolve the City of Austin as its first order of business in two days, I won't sign a single bill until that one gets through."

"The Senate will not work on anything but that, I assure you on that one," Clark Bentley responded. The lieutenant governor was reserved and spoke sparingly, but his position as head of the Senate afforded him great power in state politics. Clark was a darling of the Tea Party groups and other far right grassroots organizations. He was smart and charismatic, though somewhat unassuming in stature compared to the others in the room. He wore a nice suit and a dress shirt with no tie, except for very formal occasions. For this meeting, he had taken off the jacket and rolled up the sleeves on his shirt.

"What's our plan for the next 48 hours, Jack?" Tim asked.

"Well, SWAT and crowd control will be here within the hour as I said," Jack began. They will work 12 hour shifts and rotate out so a full complement is here 24 hours per day. I suppose we will see what happens when we hit their 48 hour ultimatum, but I will have everyone on standby and will also request Georgetown, Round Rock, and a bunch of the surrounding suburbs to be ready to assist. I assume they will not be on board with the Austin rebellion or whatever we are calling it. That is as far as we have gotten, lot more planning to do over the next day or so."

"If I can find an appropriate charge prior to them attempting to enforce this warrant, should we preempt them by making the arrest on the chief and magistrate and the City Board before the deadline?" Grace asked. "I know we can, I am asking for opinions on if we should."

"Damn right we should," Tim barked. "Hell, I'll arrest them myself if I have to."

"We can certainly do that, Grace," Jack said. "We will do it at their homes, avoid a direct conflict if possible."

Grace smiled, she appreciated Jack's demeanor. Tim was a fantastic leader as governor, but Jack was measured and prudent in a way that was rarely seen in law enforcement. No nonsense, but no unnecessary violence either.

"I'm just blowing off steam, Jack," Tim said more gently. "I know your guys will handle it. As far as the suburban police departments, any intel on where they stand on this? I don't want us inviting them into the fray only to find out they are on the wrong side."

"Good point, Tim. I will find out before we reach out to them," Jack said. "Just a thought, might want to consider calling up the National Guard, in case this spins out of control quickly. A battle with what's left of their police department is not too concerning in the grand scheme of things. But if a lot of their supporters show up...."

"Yes, we will activate the Guard immediately," Tim nodded his head. "We will get a bunch of them here to supplement your guys and a lot more on standby if needed." Having calmed down significantly, he shook head slowly and whispered, "Dear God, how did we get to this?"

3.

Ray pulled a duffle bag out from under his bed. Unzipping it, he withdrew the AK-47 rifle with its side folding stock from within. He peered into the bag to check on the ammunition available, counting a dozen magazines, each loaded with thirty rounds of hard-hitting 7.62x39 soft points. Some of the bluing was worn of the barrel and receiver, but the gun was as comfortable as ever in his hands. Ray's former police department was one of only a very few in the country that allowed the AK-47 to be carried on duty as a patrol rifle. Ray had purchased one due to the reliability of the system and the powerful cartridge it fired. He had never really been a fan of the AR-15, but wouldn't have complained if he had been issued that instead. He just preferred the simplicity and minimalist nature of the AK when given the choice.

Minimalism was a key component of Ray's life. His home was sparsely furnished by the standards of the day. A loveseat, a TV, and a desk occupied the living room. The only bedroom contained a bed and nightstand. The only other furnishings were to contain the one thing he did collect: shelves and shelves of books. Ray was an avid reader and had been since he was very young. Classics dominated his collection, but there were some modern fiction and non-fiction titles among them. Theological studies represented a significant portion. There were plenty of textbooks, most of those were from his time teaching criminal justice courses. Other than ammunition, books were the only collection he maintained.

He pulled his S&W 642 revolver from the front of his waistband and placed it on the counter. The only other gun he owned right now, a Springfield Armory 1911A1 sat on the nightstand. Nothing fancy, all of the guns were basic versions without lights or lasers or the other items that were currently popular among tactical enthusiasts. Ray like simplicity, and his weapons were simple and effective. Placing the AK-47 back into the duffle bag, he also put a first-aid kit in with the magazines. Zipping it up, he placed it next to the door. It would be coming with him to work for the foreseeable future.

Ray looked at the photo album sitting among his books and pulled it out. He leafed through the pictures slowly. The photos were all of his children, chronicling their growth to some extent, though taken at sporadic times based on life's circumstances. Ray and his ex-wife, Marie, had been divorced for two years now. Marie and the four kids lived up near Stephenville, a two and a half hour drive in good traffic. Their marriage had lasted for thirteen years, ten of those while Ray had been a cop in Illinois. The relationship had always been tumultuous, but they had stuck it out until two years ago. They both decided finally that they would be happier without each other. She despised the fact that Ray had to work to make money, and he resented leaving his job in law enforcement to pursue her dream of coming to Texas; at least that was how Ray saw it. In quiet moments, he would admit to himself that he had been mostly an absent husband and most certainly an absent father to his children. Being a cop had been the focal point of Ray's life, leaving his family a distant secondary consideration.

The separation had been good for both of them. Ray saw the kids whenever he could. Marie kept the house and they each lived their own lives. Ray was actually happier alone. He loved his children, and he missed them, but he could barely tolerate more than a few hours around Marie. It was not because Marie was in any way a bad person. For the right man she would have even been an excellent wife. Ray was not the right man, and they had very different goals and interests. Marie was a good mother to his children, and Ray reminded himself of that fact every time he became frustrated with her.

For Ray, living his own life meant mostly reading and shooting. He attended a Wing Chun class every Thursday night. An avid mixed martial artist in his younger days, Ray opted for something a little less strenuous as his age began showing. The scientific fighting style that Wing Chun represented was perfect for him. He loved the strategic precision of the art.

A small shooting range at the back of the property allowed Ray to shoot pretty regularly, and with only three guns in his armory, they each got a pretty good workout. The range consisted of steel silhouette targets, small steel plates, and a backstop made of old railroad ties that paper targets could be stapled to. Back on his old department, Ray had been a sniper on the part-time SWAT team. The need for snipers was limited, so most of his time was spent on the entry team. He liked both about equally, but his lack of a sniper rifle right now spoke to which he preferred. There was nothing like the rush of an entry. He missed it. Every time he thought of it, he resented leaving it even more. With a sigh, he leafed through a few more pictures and then picked up his phone.

Busy? He texted Marie's phone.

A minute later came the reply. *No, what's up?*

He called her number, hoping she would pick up. They spoke only occasionally, a frequency which seemed to be critical to their getting along at all.

"Hey," Marie's voice picked up.

"Hi, how are the kids doing," Ray asked.

"They're fine. Everything ok? You sound serious," she said.

"Yes, I guess, I don't know," Ray hesitated, not sure of his own next thoughts. "Just, a lot of weird stuff going on in Austin right now."

Marie laughed, "keep Austin weird, isn't that what they say?"

"Yes, but, I don't know. This is different," Ray was processing slowly as they spoke. "Listen, I want you to make sure you have your gun with you all the time now, ok?"

"I always do, but what's going on?" Marie inquired, obviously alert to his mood.

"The City Board voted to arrest the governor or some crazy shit, I barely know what to make of it. I don't think it will spread up by you in cowboy town, but just the same, people are getting crazy and you should be a little more alert than usual," Ray said in his rapid Chicago accent.

"Arrest the governor? What the hell is wrong with those people?" Marie asked.

"They're nutjobs, no other explanation," Ray responded. "Anyway, say hi to the kids for me and just stay alert."

Ray hung up before Marie could ask any more questions. Their conversations rarely ended well if they went on too long. Marie usually felt the need to recount all of Ray's perceived trespasses and Ray responded to each with accusations of his own. Short conversations were best. Ray knew Marie well enough to know she would take his advice to heart, and probably look into whatever information was available on the internet to see what he was talking about.

Ray grabbed a Milt Sparks holster for the 1911 from the drawer of his nightstand. The snub nose revolver would be relegated to an ankle holster for backup gun duty and the 1911 would be his primary gun for now. A speed strip of ammo for the revolver and extra magazine would complete his personal defense equipment until whatever was going on blew over. The AK-47 in its duffle bag would sit under his desk or in his car for extreme emergencies that required more than a handgun. Ray was not a fan of wearing a sport coat unless he needed to, especially in the Texas heat, but that would need to be a part of the routine. Although Texas allowed the open carry of firearms, Ray never saw the wisdom of doing so outside of being in a police uniform.

Pouring a glass of rum, Ray sat down with a book to finish the evening. Rum and bourbon were Ray's favorite drinks. He never over-indulged, but he regularly had a glass of one or the other before retiring for the evening. After reading a few chapters in the book, Ray realized he didn't remember anything he had just read. This was not uncommon for Ray. When his mind was preoccupied with something else, he would read without comprehending and not realize where he left off the next time he picked up the book. He put the book mark back to where he started, figuring he would need to go back and read again when he could pay attention to it. He was asleep by 10pm.

4.

Inside the sprawling interior of a steel building, over one hundred people crowded to listen to a man at a small podium who spoke with no microphone but was clearly heard by all in attendance. The private ranch in Marble Falls was a regular meeting place for the group calling themselves the Hill Country Militia Group-Section Alpha. Fifty of the faces were new, and were segregated from the main group of regular attendees.

The man at the microphone was not large, standing only a hair over five feet and six inches. His presence was still imposing. Mac McCoy was a retired Green Beret and had spent over twenty years in Army Special Forces. He was a charismatic man, a natural leader and teacher, which made him excel in his military career and also made him a leader of men in this militia. Even at forty-six years old, Mac was in incredible physical shape. For two years, Mac had been growing the size of the militia and had been training them weekly. No other Texas militia was as rigid in its training regimen as the Hill Country Militia was. Before tonight, they were fifty strong and they were becoming a fighting force to be reckoned with. Amongst the original fifty were twenty current law enforcement officers with various departments. Militia membership was by invitation only and was secret. There was no written record of anyone or anything related to the Hill Country Militia. The spoken word was the only mode of communication between members; no emails were allowed for Militia business.

"As you can see, we have some strangers among us tonight," Mac began. "They were strangers to most of us before tonight, but ten of our own members have sponsored them and tonight they become our brothers." Mac paused to let the group look over the new members. "They will, without a doubt, be excellent additions to our Militia."

The group applauded as Mac paused. He continued, "These fifty- four men were members of the Austin Police Department until just a couple of hours ago. They, along with 750 of their peers, resigned after a Declaration of Independence, some might even say a declaration of war, by the City Board that included their chief of police obtaining a warrant for the arrest of our governor."

The crowd murmured in disbelief. "That's right, those communist bastards in Austin think they are going to arrest our governor in 48 hours. I am thinking that the Hill Country Militia Group just might have something to say about that!"

The crowd erupted in cheers and chants of "Come and take it!"

As it died down, Mac continued. "Please welcome these fine officers into our brotherhood. I know they haven't had time to train with us, but they all have lengthy experience as cops, know their way around a gun, and more importantly, know their way around Austin. I am assigning each of you to partner with them. As of this moment, men, we are operational!"

As the hooting and hollering died down, the new members were given uniforms consisting of green ATAC-S camouflage BDU's and matching boonie hats. There were no insignia on the uniforms, and no name tags. All of the Militia's weapons were personally owned, the only requirements being a rifle in 5.56mm and a handgun in .45acp. Monthly dues, paid in cash by each member, covered the cost of uniforms and ammunition. The quartermaster handed out boxes of ammunition to each member, a case of 5.56mm and four boxes of .45acp for each.

Half of the former Austin police officers in the group had at least some SWAT experience, all of them excelled in shooting and were in good physical condition. More than anyone in the room except perhaps Mac, they seemed anxious to jump into this fray. The fringe element of the community they served had abandoned them, as had their department. Taking it back was not outside their hopes.

The groups partnered up and sat down to get to know each other while loading magazines for their pistols and rifles. The mood was light, but there was little doubt among them that this was about to become deadly serious. Everyone was aware of what had happened in Austin, and the former officers shared plenty of stories form the past several weeks about what had been going on there.

Mac invited one of the new recruits, a former commander with Austin PD, to speak for a moment. The commander gave an emotional recounting of his career, of his brothers and sisters in blue, and of the recent demise of the agency. He also gave intel on equipment, the size of the remaining force, locations of substations, and a variety of other valuable information. He thanked the militia members for their patriotism and for the welcoming that he and his brothers received.

Mac resumed his position at the podium about an hour later, allowing the new members and veteran members to mingle and get to know each other. Behind him was a chalkboard that he used to establish each 12-man team's area of responsibility. The plan was for the group to go home tonight and get some rest and regroup at dusk in the barn tomorrow. They would receive a group text using codes if they were to stand down or if they were to deploy sooner. Outside of that, they would be filtering into the city by dusk and in place and ready for the potential problems as the deadline for the governor to evacuate the governor's mansion approached.

"What happens here will go down in our nation's history, gentlemen," Mac said somberly. "Most certainly, the next few days will determine the future of Texas, and I am proud to be a part of this with you. If it be God's will, I pray this great state will carry on and this moment will be but a footnote in a history book, that two days from now the day will pass with but a whimper from the opposition. But if it be His will that fighting should be done, then we will bring a fight to this event that will never be forgotten."

The crowd shouted "Amen!" Handshakes and hugs concluded the night's events and the Militia dispersed for the evening.

5.

Ray grabbed his briefcase and slung the duffle bag over his shoulder as he got out of the Highlander in the parking garage. It was still dark at 6:30am when he started the walk down 9th Street to Congress. He could see the graffiti from across the street at he approached the Liberty Policy Foundation. The light gray exterior concrete was spray painted with black swastikas inside red circles with a line drawn through them, six of them in all. The words "Nazis go home" were painted on the glass doors.

Ray paused across the street to look around. No one seemed to be in the area and there didn't appear to be any damage to the doors or windows other than the spray paint. He cautiously approached the front door, used his key card to unlock it, and slipped inside. He made a quick interior check to make sure all the ground floor doors were locked and intact.

Ray took the stairs to his office on the third floor and sent an email to the CEO of the foundation from his computer explaining last night's meeting and detailing the graffiti on the building he discovered this morning. He recommended that all personnel be advised to work from home for a couple of days to see how this all played out. Ray placed the duffle bag under his desk and went to get a glass of water from the kitchen area. When he returned, the CEO's response was waiting in his inbox:

"Ray, thank you for the concern. With all due respect for your experience, the Foundation does not expect to be cowered into absence. We will work from the office as usual and use appropriate diligence in looking for possible danger.-Dave"

Ray grumbled briefly, then decided against a reply. Dave Johnson was new to the Foundation, coming from academia before landing there. He was a good man, but oblivious to the realities of the world as many academics can tend to be. As a conservative, Dave was already rare among academics and Ray was thankful for at least this much. Common street smarts would have been too much to expect. He did respect that Dave was courageous in his pursuit of conservatism, but this was not an act of courage for anyone who truly understood the possible danger here. Courage without prudence was recklessness.

Ray unzipped the duffle bag and inserted one of the magazines into the AK-47, but did not chamber a round. While hoping he would not need to use it, he gave the weapon a quick inspection to make sure it was in the same condition he last left it in. Confident that it was, he placed it back in the bag under his desk, but left it unzipped.

The third floor analysts were slow to come in, which was not unusual, but there were fewer than normal arriving. Each arrival brought new intelligence with them about a gathering crowd on the street. By 9:30, all those who were coming to the office had arrived, but most of the employees sat looking out their windows and not doing any work. Groups of the analysts gathered in the offices with a view of the street to look down at the gathering protestors and spoke to each other in whispers.

Ray pondered the likely reality that the graffiti out front was more than just damaging and harassing, it was marking a target for the coming mob. He considered talking to Dave by phone and telling him that everyone should leave, now. He decided it would be fruitless and thought about just leaving anyway. It was a fleeting thought, he knew he wouldn't leave the rest of them here alone. Ray knew that he should have been more assertive in his recommendation, but now he would have to deal with the situation as it developed. There was no use in looking back.

By 10am, the chanting from the street could be heard throughout the building. Ray found it difficult to determine what was being said, but there were a limited number of chants used by the mobs and it was probably one of those. As he sat staring blankly at his computer screen, Dave came into his office and closed the door.

"I might have made a mistake in not listening to you, Ray," he began. Dave was not arrogant, and it was obvious he knew that he was wrong. Ray was not one to remind him of it either.

"Dave, it's ok. But we should get everyone out now," Ray told him. "If we go out the back door into the alley in groups of ten, I can drive everyone and drop them off at the parking garages in the company van. We should do that now, before the streets get blocked off."

There were two parking garages used by the Foundation and they were in opposite directions, but neither was more than few blocks from the building. Ray thought the entire movement should only take about fifteen minutes to get everyone to their cars.

"Ray, whatever you think is best," Dave nodded, noticeably nervous. "The crowds are gathering out front, not right in front of the building but not far away either."

"The graffiti marks this place as a target, Dave. Once it starts we will get hit," Ray said, a seriousness on his face that was uncharacteristic from Dave's knowledge of him. "If you can gather everyone on the second floor we can split into groups based on which parking garage they are in and get going, I'll drive groups of ten or so to the garages and drop them off."

Before Dave could answer him an alarm went off in the building and over the loudspeaker came a scream from the intern at the front desk downstairs. "Intruders!" was all she said.

6.

Mac had slept well and was giving a final cleaning to his weapons. His partner was next to him going over his Remington 700. Seth Pearson was a retired police SWAT sniper from Fort Worth police department. Seth was mild mannered and detail oriented, like most police snipers. He raised chickens and goats on his ranch outside Marble Falls now, a big change from being a big city police officer, but a welcome one. He had been involved in two shootings during his time as a cop, one in patrol and one as a sniper responding to a hostage situation. Mac trusted him, knowing he been tested, and the two were close friends.

Decentralized by design, leadership was not fully identifiable, but if there was a second person in charge of the Militia behind Mac, it would be Seth. Mac looked over at him and simply said, "Thoughts?"

"I think a fight is coming to Austin," Seth said after taking a deep breath. "I think we should be in it."

"I agree," Mac said, nodding his head slowly. "My question is more about what we discussed before."

"You mean, are we willing to kick it off?" Seth asked.

"Yes," Mac said. "Are we willing to kick it off?

Seth loaded four rounds of .300 Winchester Magnum match grade ammunition into the rifle, the only member authorized for such a weapon. Propping the rifle up on its buttstock on the table in front of him, he held it upright by its barrel and leaned on it slightly. The position of his arm exposing the large III% tattoo on his forearm. "I am," he said after a brief hesitation.

"Good," Mac replied. "So am I. How do you think the others will react?"

"They are good group, Mac. Not one will shy away from a fight," Seth paused. "But, I think they don't need to know the details of how that fights starts or who starts it. These new Austin guys, they are ready for war, I know that much. They are fighting to take back their city, there won't be any hesitation in that bunch. "

"Agreed," Mac said, patting his partner on the shoulder. The indigenous fighters Mac had embedded with to train in Afghanistan were not always reliable. These men were all Americans. They were different races and ethnicities, but they were all Americans. There was little question about their reliability. And Seth was right about the recent influx of the recently departed Austin cops, they were a serious bunch and had reason to want this fight more than any of the others.

The difference between this fight and the one overseas was the fact that the enemies here were also Americans. Maybe not cut from the same cloth as these men, certainly they would not be as skilled either. But the killing here, whichever side it occurred on, would be of Americans and by Americans. This was new even for the most experienced veterans. Mac momentarily wondered how long it would take to get used to killing Americans. In that regard, some of the police officers on the team had more experience than anyone else, though each would say they never got used to it. Mac was used to killing, so were others on the team with time overseas. The combination of the experiences with his law enforcement guys and military guys was a benefit as he saw it. Still, this was new territory for everyone.

Seth gently cleaned the lenses on his 5-20x Nightforce scope before closing the scope covers and putting in his drag bag. With the padded partition, he slid his AR-15 into the other side of the bag. The sniper rifle was a precision instrument capable of delivering accurate firepower at extreme distances, but was next to useless in a close quarter situation, which is why he brought the AR-15. Seth sat down on a chair to enjoy the morning air, sipped on a large cup of coffee, and stared out over the hills of Texas under the midmorning sun.

7.

Jack walked into Tim's office without bothering to knock. "I told Grace and Clark and the staffers to work from home for a couple of days. Only one here is your secretary, she got in before I could tell her. I am having one of troopers drive her home pretty soon. Hope that's ok with you?"

"Yes, that was a good idea," Tim nodded, motioning for Jack to sit in the chair in front of his desk. "We are going to make a stand here, but they don't need to be in the middle of it, makes no difference really and I would rather not have to worry about their safety."

"I attached a security detail to both of them for now," Jack replied. He paused for a minute before starting again. "Tim, I know making a stand is important, I agree with you on that," he paused again as Tim lowered his reading glasses and leaned closer to listen to him. "Just thinking out loud though, what if we got you out of here secretly and made our stand with you being somewhere secure?"

Tim leaned back, exhaling loudly as he clasped his hands in front of his chest. "Are you kidding me?" he replied.

"No, and I knew you would say that," Jack replied. "But it don't make a darn bit of difference in the optics if you are actually here or if everyone just thinks you are. Let my guys make the stand, that's why they are here. We can get you through the tunnels in the capitol and out the back and jump in a car, no would see us."

"I appreciate you, Jack" Tim spoke slowly and earnestly. "I know what you mean, but I am not going anywhere."

"Alright, then," Jack started, "let's go over the initial strategy." Jack knew there was no way Tim would leave, but felt obligated to suggest it. "I don't think we are going to avoid a fight here tomorrow, Tim."

"We aren't going to be able to, Jack. This is something different than ever before though, and I don't intend to pull any punches and let anyone think this is going to be acceptable ever again," Tim said. His eyes focused like a laser on Jack, his intention unmistakable. "Grace is ready to defend this administration and all of the troopers in any court proceedings that might follow, tell those men and women to just do the right thing and they will be fine."

"The right thing is getting harder and harder to define these days, Tim," Jack responded with a long exhale. "Defending this capitol, defending you, defending the Legislative Session though, those are the right things. Of that much, I am sure."

8.

Dave froze temporarily, overwhelmed by the scream and the alarm. Ray immediately pulled the AK-47 from his bag and snapped open the stock. As he moved to the door of his office he charged the bolt and chambered a round with a distinct *ca-chunk*. He looked at Dave and said, "Dave, I need you to get everyone onto the second floor. Get everyone off of three, four, five, and six, I will take care of the first floor. Start dividing them into groups like we discussed by parking garage locations."

Dave was wide-eyed, but started moving toward the door. The building used a security system to secure the three floors that the analysts worked on, blocking the elevators and the doors from the stairwells from opening without a passkey. The other floors were accessible by either elevator or stairwell, and it was not uncommon for analysts to venture up to the 6th floor balcony to enjoy the sun while working on their computers. Dave moved quickly to round up his team.

Ray ran to the stairwell, bounding down to the second floor where he went out to an adjoining stairwell that opened into a broad, richly wooded staircase to the lobby. He flipped down the safety lever on his rifle and slowed down as he approached the lobby area, now visible from the wide staircase. Three masked men were moving about in front of the reception desk, the farthest one was busy spray painting the walls with more anti-Nazi and anarchist symbols. The second man was pouring gasoline from a can onto the area rug and the front desk. The third glared menacingly at the young intern, who was behind the desk but pressed into the wall as far as she could go, her face frozen in terror.

"GET OUT!" Ray commanded in his former cop voice. All three flinched and turned their attention to him. The third intruder glared at him raising his hand to expose a Zippo lighter.

"You Nazis love your fossil fuels, don't you?" he sneered through a scarf that covered his mouth. A large 'A' in a circle, the anarchists' symbol, was emblazoned in red on the front of his black hoodie. "Enjoy it now," he laughed and flipped open the lighter's lid with a metallic click.

Dave centered the front sight post on the tip of the 'A' in the symbol on the hoodie and squeezed the trigger without hesitation. He didn't feel the recoil, or hear the shot, but he saw the intruder crumple to the floor. The other two ran for the front door as Ray tracked them with the front sight post. They scrambled to squeeze through the hole they had smashed in the bottom portion of the door and he waited for them to be completely out before turning his attention to the intern.

"Dial 911," he said. "Tell them we've had intruders who attempted an arson and there has been a shooting, and…" he looked at her and saw she was in shock, her eyes glued to the body on the floor. "Amber!" Ray yelled to get her attention.

She looked at him, eyes wide. "Amber, dial 911, tell them we had a break in and there has been a shooting," Ray's voice sounded distant to himself, but there was no ringing in his ears yet. A high powered rifle in an enclosed space was particularly bad for the human ear, but the adrenaline had kept him from hearing it.

As the intern started to dial 911, Ray pushed a couch from the lobby in front of the hole in the glass of the front door and then backed it up with a bookcase. He did not want anyone else coming through, or maybe throwing a lighter into the gasoline saturated lobby. Outside he saw that the crowd had mostly dispersed, not because of the shooting, but because they were attacking other specific businesses in small groups. There were scattered men and women in dark clothing and hoodies all down Congress, all the way up to the front of the capitol.

Ray heard the phone placed back into its cradle. Turning to Amber he asked, "What did they say, did they give you a response time?"

Amber's eyes were wide. In disbelief she said, "They told me 'sorry, we don't help Nazis,' and hung up on me. The police just hung up on me."

Ray looked at her for a moment, also in disbelief. "Ok, Amber, go up to my office on the third floor and grab the duffle bag under my desk and bring it down. Tell Dave to send the first group down, they should be gathering on the second floor." Ray watched her go to the elevator and then moved around behind the desk to get the keys to the van.

It appeared that the trio that had attacked the Foundation were not going to be reinforced right away. Maybe they had figured a building full of conservative academic types wouldn't push back too much while they burned down the building, and three would be enough. Maybe there just weren't enough of these hoodlums to go around. Either way, Ray was sure they would return at some point. This time they would come with guns, knowing he had already shot one of them. It was time to get everyone out.

Ray walked over to the lifeless body on the floor. He looked at the man's unblinking eyes, staring at nothing. He reached down and removed the scarf covering the lower half of his face. Searching his own feelings, he found none. The dead man was ugly, and dead. That was about it. Ray questioned whether or not this lack of remorse was normal. Shootings involving police officers being rare, Ray had never been involved in a one during his entire career as a police officer despite all of the arrests and SWAT raids he was involved in. He had always wondered how he would feel if he were involved in one, but never doubted that he would do it if he needed to. Throughout his career he had come to the conclusion that so long as it was a righteous shooting, he didn't anticipate it would bother him. He had now proven himself correct, it didn't bother him at all.

The elevator doors behind him opened and a group came out. Gasps and covered mouths followed the discovery of violence that had been but a few short minutes ago combined with the overwhelming odor of gasoline. Amber struggled with the weight of the duffle bag and handed it to Ray, who promptly slung the shoulder strap over his back. Spinning it to the front of his body, he retrieved an extra magazine and tucked it into his waistband.

He motioned the group to head for the alley door and turned to Dave for a moment. "If you can have the rest of them ready, I will call you when I am approaching the rear door. How many are there in total?"

"There are just two groups, thankfully a lot of the analysts decided to stay home today," Dave seemed a little relieved to be able to say. "If you just come back to pick this group up, we can head to the Colorado garage. You can leave the van there and head home too, Ray. Don't risk coming back to drop the van off and walking back."

Ray smiled at Dave, he was finally understanding the situation and making good decisions. "Yes, sir. I will be back here shortly."

Ray folded the stock on his AK-47 and partially concealed it under his sport coat, slipping out the side door to the passenger van parked in front of the building. Sliding into the driver's seat, he started the van and rested the rifle next to his right knee, muzzle on the floor board. The rifle would fire in the folded position, and was more maneuverable in the confines of a vehicle this way.

Ray pulled away from the curb and made the immediate left into the alley as the back door opened and the group of ten of his co-workers piled into the van. Picking up speed through the alley, Ray swerved out into the street and was in front of the parking garage in a few moments. Pulling in front of the door to the garage entrance, he scanned the area for signs of rioters and saw none.

"Those of you with friends or family outside of Austin might want to consider heading that way instead of staying here if you have that option. Things are going to get ugly here soon, be as far away as you can." The group thanked him as they got out of the van and headed to their cars. Ray was sure they would not heed his advice, and that the ones who lived in the city, which was most of them, would head straight home and wait for this to all blow over. While most of them were expert statisticians in their fields of policy, he hoped they were right in their calculation of the risk they would face by staying.

Ray pulled away from the garage and raced back to the Foundation. He tore down the alley and saw that the back door was ajar, and two rioters were fighting with the group to get the door open, struggling back and forth as the team of policy analysts and interns tried to push them out the door and get it closed. As he skidded to a stop and jumped out of the van, Ray snapped the stock back into place and brought the rifle up to his line of sight. "GET BACK!" he barked at them. The tone of his voice turned them toward him. "I SAID GET BACK!"

The two stopped fighting for the door and it was immediately closed from within, but they held their ground. Ray did not consider this to be war yet, so he was hesitant to shoot them without a perceived deadly threat. They glared at him and the one closest to him hissed, "we don't listen to Nazis."

Ray may have yielded on deadly force, but felt no obligation to use what would normally be reasonable force either. He briskly closed the distance between them and smashed the butt of his rifle into the bridge of the closest man's nose, collapsing him to the ground. Blood gushed out of his nose as he cursed at Ray and covered it with his hand. The second man turned and ran down the alley. As the first man went to all fours to get back up, blood dripping on the pavement below him, Ray crashed the butt of the rifle into the back of the man's head, knocking him unconscious.

Ray slapped the back of the door with an open hand, yelling, "It's ok, it's Ray. Come on out, we have to get going."

The group of eight were the remaining employees and they all piled into the van that Ray had left running during the brief melee. He folded the stock again, jumped in and raced through the alley toward the garage on Colorado. The drive was brief and as the van pulled up to curb, Ray gave this group the same advice he gave to the last. Dave turned to Ray and extended his hand. They wished one another well and headed for their cars. Ray was on the road in minutes, heading for the highway and away from the craziness of the city. He dialed 911 from his cellphone.

"State police, 911, what is your emergency?" came the voice of the dispatcher.

"My name, is Ray Tucker, I was involved in a shooting on Congress Avenue in Austin," Ray began.

"Is anyone injured?" came the calm response.

"Yes, one man is dead, Austin Police refused to respond," Ray explained.

"You will need to report this to Austin PD, sir, it is their jurisdiction," the emotionless voice responded.

"I just told you, I tried," Ray insisted.

"Then you've done what you need to sir, have a nice day," the voice said and the phone disconnected.

Ray looked at his phone in disbelief. This was insane. This was not how police departments act, not how civil society acts. He put the phone on the seat next to him and pressed to 90 miles per hour. Who really cared at this point?

9.

A large group of Austin police officers were gathered outside the perimeter of the governor's mansion. They were mostly standing by their patrol cars, talking amongst each other. More were arriving in groups, shuttled by a transport van from headquarters.

The DPS troopers had ringed the mansion earlier than they anticipated given the 48 hour notice the Austin police chief had proclaimed. They had with them shields, not the usual riot shields but rather ballistic resistant shields based on this unprecedented potential confrontation with other uniformed police officers, some of whom still had guns. Besides the Austin patrol officers, groups of protestors in hoodies and masks were also arriving.

Tim looked out at the street from the window in his office. "Do you have enough people, Jack?" he said without turning away, "the Guard won't be here until tomorrow at the earliest."

"I have more on the way, I don't like the looks of this," Jack said as he peered over Tim's shoulder out to the street below.

Jack's phone rang and he stepped away to take the call. Tim glared out the window. He had a seething hatred for the Austin police officers down below, more than for the protestors. Protestors were a dime a dozen, moving from one social justice cause to another without any thought given. They were misguided youths, he thought, that would grow out of it one day for the most part. But the cops, they swore an oath, and this was not part of it. This was a betrayal of the highest order in his eyes. Tim still identified with cops more than anything else. It was one of the reasons he was so close with Jack. Cops were still heroes in his eyes, and this was an unforgivable evil as far as he was concerned.

"Tim, we just got some strange news," Jack's voice brought Tim around to face him. "Fusion center out in Albuquerque sent information on a caravan of about ten touring buses, all black, heading west on 40."

"Ok, what makes it interesting," Tim asked.

"They were traveling in a caravan and an Albuquerque patrol unit tried to make a traffic stop on the last bus, mostly to see who and what they were given they didn't have any license plates, and they refused to stop. Never even changed speed, just kept going," Jack said.

"So they just let them go?" Tim asked incredulously.

"Albuquerque PD is still under a federal consent decree from the last administration, part of it includes a 'no pursuit' policy. They had to pull off. Anyway, they will be approaching the border shortly, Fusion is trying to locate satellite data to see where they originated from, but nothing yet," Jack said. "I have a State Police air unit on the way to monitor them."

"Check with Amarillo and see if they have units available to make a stop, let these people know that Texas is not a 'no pursuit policy' kind of place," Tim said with a grin. "Think it could be feds, or military?"

"Could be, but they would probably have yielded to local law enforcement, right?" Jack responded.

"I would think so, even if they couldn't tell them what they were doing or where they were going. Pulling this kind of crap draws more attention than just complying briefly," Tim said.

"We'll monitor it," Jack said.

10.

Sergeant Rutherford stood at the podium for roll call and was handed a piece of paper from a dispatcher who popped her head into the room briefly. He peered down through his reading glasses at the message from the Fusion Center in New Mexico.

"Russel, Tomkins, and Davis. The three of you load up your squads and start heading west on 40," he looked out at the room full of patrolmen. "Info on a caravan of buses heading eastbound our way, didn't stop for Albuquerque PD apparently and there's some suspicion about who they are or where they're from. DPS has an air unit enroute, but most of their road guys are moving toward Austin for that nonsense they got going on down there," he smirked a little while saying the last part. "Let us know if you need more people. Just head west until you see them, you can go out of town. DPS is requesting the assistance."

The three patrol officers grabbed their bags and walked to the squad parking lot. They asked each other what this was about and each concluded with a shrug. They were westbound on 40 in about five minutes, changing channels to communicate with the DPS helicopter that was headed toward them.

"Air One to Alpha 6-2, how do you copy?" the pilot's voice crackled over Officer Russel's lapel mic.

"Alpha 6-2 to Air One, you are loud and clear. Alpha 6-7 and Alpha 6-8 are with me, we are westbound 40 exiting the city limits and looking for the caravan," Russel relayed.

"Air One, copy. We are just ahead of you, will advise when the caravan is in sight," came the reply.

The trio of squad cars edged over 100 miles per hour through the open highway, awaiting visual confirmation from the air unit as they left the Amarillo city limits behind them.

11.

"There is a lot of activity out there, Jack," Tim said, standing back by the window. "Their 48 hour warning seems to have been abbreviated."

Jack looked out the window next to Tim. He pulled a tin of Copenhagen from his pocket and offered some to Tim. Tim took a pinch as did Jack and both looked out at the gathering crowds. "I don't think this is going to wait until tomorrow," Jack said slowly.

The crowd was intermingling with the Austin police officers, loud music was playing and many were dancing, including some of the officers. Tim noticed that a lot of the Austin cops weren't carrying guns. That had slipped his attention earlier, most likely being drawn away by the untucked uniform shirts some of the officers sported.

"What's with the cops not having guns?" he asked Jack.

"Chief Wilshire, he…she, whatever, made it optional recently," Jack said. "Their new hires for the most part were anti-gun types. Some of them refused to shoot in the academy and don't even have their certifications because of it."

"What the hell?" Tim looked at him.

"Things have been spiraling in that department for years, but ever since this new chief came in it has been a real circus," Jack said. "The City Board hated the cops, so they hired a chief that hates cops and a bunch of new cops that hate cops. Pretty much sums it up."

As more groups sporadically showed up, they edged closer to the perimeter the DPS officers had formed.

Tim sat down at his desk and pointed for Jack to have a seat as well. He dialed his secretary and asked her to have Grace and Clark call in on his conference line, after which she was to go home with the security escort Jack offered earlier. After a few moments, his phone beeped to let him know both were on the line.

"Grace, Clark, y'all there?" He spoke into the speakerphone.

Both acknowledged they were.

"I got Jack here with me, just wanted to update everyone," Tim began. "There is a pretty good crowd outside the mansion, including a bunch of Austin PD personnel. It looks like a street party down there. Jack and I are pretty sure that this isn't going to wait until tomorrow to start, whatever that means. Stay away from here for the time being, we will keep you posted."

"Tim, I hate not being there," Clark said.

"I know, Clark," Tim said. "I know you would be here if I let you, which is why I am ordering you not to be here."

"Tim, I am meeting with my staff tomorrow out in McLennan County to go over options for prosecuting the regime there in Austin," Grace said.

"McLennan County?" Tim asked.

"Yes, we are looking into charging outside of Travis or Williamson County based on what is going on, this is nearly an open rebellion and we haven't got indication one way or the other where the Austin-area counties stand on this," she replied.

"Ok, good idea," Tim said.

"Your security details ok Grace, Clark?" Jack asked.

"Yes, Jack, your people are always true professionals, thank you for sending them," Clark answered.

"Same here," Grace said.

"Ok, you two keep your heads down and we will talk soon," Tim said before disconnecting.

12.

Ray poured a healthy dose of George Dickel No.8 into a rocks glass and put his AK-47 on the counter. His hands were steady, he felt no remorse for the violence he had brought upon those rioters. Whiskey or rum were a nightly routine for Ray but not a method of self-medicating. He genuinely liked drinking the spirits, and although this was a lot earlier in the day than he usually had his glass it seemed warranted under the circumstances. Ray genuinely felt bad for those officers who struggled horribly in the aftermath of a shooting, but he was sure that he would not be one of those that did. The shooting today was clearly justified, that maniac was trying to burn down a building full of people. He had no regrets about doing it. The whiskey was just something he enjoyed, not something he needed.

The part of the shooting that concerned him was that it was already over, everything was apparently already over. There wasn't even a police report on the matter. Ray had investigated officer-involved shootings in his time as a detective, and even a couple of self-defense shootings by private citizens. The process was long and detailed, without exception. This was like something out of the movies where there is a shooting and then the rest of the day's activities continue on like nothing ever happened. This was exactly like that, and it bothered him.

Ray took a sip of whiskey, the buttery smooth texture giving way to the heat as he began to swallow it. He picked up his cell phone and sent a text to Marie.

Everything going ok by you guys?

He was not in the mood to talk to her, and didn't really want to have to explain what had happened at this moment. A few minutes passed, a few more sips of the amber liquid.

All good, you?

Yes, all good.

Ray took the AK-47 from its bag. There was some blood on the buttstock from the last rioter, and he rinsed it in the kitchen sink before spraying it with some bleach. He sprayed some bleach in the bag as well. Though far from phobic about germs, Ray nonetheless was not fond of other people's blood on his things.

He took another sip of whiskey and then pulled out a couple of duck eggs from the fridge along with some bacon and began heating up the cast iron skillet on the stove. Flipping on the news, he saw live footage of a crowd gathering around the governor's mansion. State troopers in riot gear were in formation around the perimeter of the mansion. Ray scrambled the eggs, adding a little splash of cream, while the bacon cooked on the skillet, then transferred them to the skillet once the bacon was done. He used the bacon grease to cook the eggs in. Once they were done, he took his plate and sat down in front of the television to watch as the live coverage continued. The duck eggs were bigger, richer, and a little creamier than chicken eggs, and Ray's ex-wife kept him with a good supply of them from her small flock. Marie didn't care for duck eggs at all, and would never dream of using them for meat, but she liked having the ducks. It worked out well for both of them, and the ducks.

On the television, Ray watched the party-like atmosphere of the rioters, including the way they interacted with Austin police officers. There was almost no difference between them. He noticed some of the cops weren't wearing guns, and thought it was odd to see their shirts untucked with no gun-belts on. They looked like they were in the locker room after a shift ended rather than actively patrolling.

As he finished eating his meal and stood to bring the plate to the sink, the screen showed a large black limousine pull in front of the crowd. The camera zoomed in as an Austin police officer got out of the driver's side and opened the rear door. Chief Wilshire ungracefully extracted herself form the rear of the limousine to a roaring crowd. She waved her hands at the crowd, one containing a piece of paper and another a megaphone. Reporters swarmed to her with microphones.

"I have an amended warrant, Mr. Leland," she barked into the megaphone in the direction of the governor's mansion, "you have three hours to vacate what is now City of Austin property. Nazis do not deserved 48 hours." The crowd erupted in cheers and chants, even the reporters were clapping.

Ray sat back down. A warrant? For the governor? Ray supposed it was of some comfort that it wasn't just him and the Foundation that were considered Nazis, the governor was painted in that light as well. Although the charge of Nazi or racist had lost most of its edge the past few years, the progressive Left still used the term to describe anyone who disagreed with them. Both terms had been used so often, under such ridiculous circumstances that they no longer had any meaning. A conservative blogger, who was also Jewish, had been labeled a Nazi by some progressive leftists because he opposed abortion. Black conservatives were called racists by leftists, not for anything relating to race but rather as a way to accuse them of abandoning their own race by becoming conservatives. The #Walkaway movement made black conservatives targets for the hurling of the same insults that were once solely reserved for white supremacists despite the fact that the fastest growing segment of the conservative movement was among the black community. Not so long ago, the terms of racist, bigot, or Nazi, were horrible insults, and being labeled either would end a political career. Now the terms held no meaning at all, other than disagreement with the Left.

Ray's eyes were glued to the screen as the crowd slowly worked itself into a frenzy. More DPS troopers came from within the mansion and they pulled back the perimeter enough to be tightened. The troopers were now standing shield to shield like the Spartans at Thermopylae. Riot batons in hand and M-4's strapped to their backs, the troopers were a long way from the Spartans with their swords and spears in terms of weapons, but not so far at all in terms of spirit or situation.

13.

"Alpha 6-2 from Air One, do you copy?" Officer Russel's radio crackled.

"Alpha 6-2 copy, go ahead Air One," he said into the mic.

"What's your location, Alpha 6-2?" the pilot asked.

"Mile marker 268, still westbound," Officer Russel responded.

"That caravan is ten miles ahead of you, 75 miles per hour, you will see them shortly," the pilot advised.

"Copy that Air One," Russel acknowledged.

The three Amarillo squads pulled into a break in the median designed as a turn-around for emergency vehicles. They sat side by side, awaiting the arrival of the mysterious convoy. Through open squad windows they spoke without the use of the radios, and finalized their plan. Officer Russel would pull out eastbound as soon as they had a visual on the caravan in order to get in front of them. The other two officers would pull in behind the group after it passed them and would initiate a traffic stop while Russel slowed down to force the lead bus to also stop. This would allow them to stop the whole convoy at once.

The convoy appeared in the distance, the flat terrain of west Texas allowing a long view. The black buses appeared as a single unit from the distance, like a slow moving cobra. As they closed, Russel pulled his squad out onto the highway and turned on his overhead lights. He accelerated to about 35 mph and weaved back and forth to signal the buses to slow down. As the buses passed, the two other squads turned on their overhead lights and sirens and pulled in behind the last bus.

Russel looked in his rearview mirror and saw the buses fast approaching. He accelerated a little to give them some room to stop as he continued to serpentine down the highway. They did not slow down. As the string of buses quickly closed on him, he realized too late that they were not going to yield at all. He swung the squad to the right to get to the shoulder, but the lead bus clipped his rear bumper as it passed, sending him into an uncontrolled spin off the road. His squad tumbled sideways, crashing into the ditch and landing on its roof, knocking Russel unconscious.

Both squads following the convoy saw Russel's squad go off the road, and hesitated in deciding whether to stop for him and let the air unit overhead follow or to continue their pursuit. Before they could radio in what happened the windows on both sides of the rear two buses opened. Three LAWS rockets fired almost simultaneously, disintegrated both squad cars and sending Air One crashing to the earth in a fiery ball. The windows on the buses closed and the serpent slithered along the road without pause, veering south on 385. The tail of the snake, the last two buses, continued east toward Amarillo.

14.

Jack hung up the phone and gave Tim a puzzled look. "Fusion Center in Albuquerque just said they used satellite footage to track back that caravan."

"And where did it originate," Tim asked, seeing as Jack had paused long enough.

"California National Guard base in Los Angeles," Jack said.

"Do we know if they are doing some sort of exercise or something?" Tim asked.

"Texas National Guard called them and they said they weren't, denied any knowledge of a convoy of buses even being at their base," Jack said.

Tim buzzed his secretary and asked her to get the governor's office in California on the line. Tim hated the California governor. Dante Malone was a progressive leftist of the highest order. During his campaign, Dante had maligned Texas and Texans repeatedly, even threatening to ban future commerce between the states if the "bathroom bill" were to become law in Texas. Malone also famously campaigned on banning ICE from California as well as ignoring federal laws and Supreme Court decisions that did not align with progressive philosophy. It was the first major win for the Democrat Socialists of America, having taken a few House seats but holding no statewide offices before his election to governor. His success had emboldened other members of the party to run separately from the Democratic Party on their own tickets, and another DSA candidate was currently poised to take the gubernatorial election in New York.

The phone on Tim's desk beeped to let him know he was connected. A voice on the other end was not Malone's.

"This is Julie Taylor, Governor Malone's chief of staff, what can I do for you Governor Leland," the voice on the line asked.

"Julie, is Dante around? This really should go through him directly," Tim responded, controlling his agitation.

"No, he isn't, but I am sure I can help you with whatever…"

Tim interrupted her midsentence, "You had a convoy of buses leave one of your Guard bases, it is probably in Texas now or close. What is it and what is it doing? Can you help with that?"

"I am sure I can't, I have no knowledge of what you are asking about," the reply was perhaps condescending, or perhaps Tim just perceived it to be.

"Which is why I asked for Dante, specifically," Tim snapped back. "Tell him to call me, immediately." Tim slammed the receiver down. Jack looked at him with understanding in his eyes. Before he could speak, Tim growled, "That state is nothing but a bunch of assholes, and that governor is king of them."

"We will deal with the convoy, Tim, but he should give us a heads up if it is headed into our jurisdiction," Jack said. "The national media is all over this Austin thing, so he knows we are dealing with crap already, no need to add to the drama."

"I don't trust him as far as I could throw that scrawny bastard," Tim growled.

15.

Ray opened his laptop and turned it on, still watching the riot brewing on the television while he waited for it to boot up. He opened the file containing his latest policy paper. This one described the rise of the socialist and anarchist movement and the coming collapse of the Democrat party. He was doing a final edit before publishing, but paused to consider that he wasn't sure when anyone from the Foundation would be returning to work. Still, the paper was a good way to occupy his mind while he peripherally monitored the scene on the news.

Ray read through his analysis again, chronicling the timing of three particular events leading up to the current political landscape. The first occurred when the current president was elected. Running a completely unorthodox Republican campaign, he had gathered support from areas that the Democrats had long controlled, such as Wisconsin, and all of the usual swing states. Boisterous and even crass at time, he appealed to a wide range of voters who considered him a refreshing departure from politics as usual. His win was not predicted by any of the polls, and the leftists and progressives in the Democratic Party were apoplectic.

The federal political scene had been in chaos since. The Democrats, a minority in both chambers of Congress, mounted a resistance campaign that simply aimed to stop anything the President tried to do. Supreme Court nominations became a circus, but in two years the President had been able to get two nominees to the bench, both of them Constitutional Orginalists in their jurisprudence. A short time later, *Alvarez v Texas* overturned the longstanding precedent case of *Roe v* Wade, and more broadly than anyone had imagined. Rather than allowing the states to decide, as the Texas case would suggest, the Court placed a prohibition on all abortion, with no exceptions. Progressive strongholds like California were even more outraged at this decision than at the results of the election. California in particular openly announced it would adopt a nullification position, ignoring Supreme Court decisions or federal legislation it did not agree with. Legislation came to grinding halt. Even criminal justice reform, a policy position near and dear to the Left, was refused to be worked on in any manner of bipartisanship. The Administration's policies in Washington DC were so deferential to state sovereignty that it did not engage the rogue states that defied the Supreme Court decisions or the federal laws in any meaningful way. The rule of law began to break down at the national level.

The second event was even more unexpected. Called the #walkaway movement, the black community began to abandon the Democrats as a reliable voting bloc. Moving up to a 35% approval among black voters, the new president was the most popular Republican politician in decades among this usually Democrat-leaning demographic. The lowest unemployment rates among African Americans in history was a driver of this popularity, and the Democrats abandonment of criminal justice reform was not far behind.

Lastly, the Hispanic vote went Republican by a solid majority in the midterm elections. This devastated the Democrats, costing them seats in Congress and in all many of the state legislatures as well. Attributed to the immigration policy debate, the Democrats has erroneously thought that all Hispanics would be pro-amnesty for illegal immigrants and proponents of their open borders policies. Legal immigrants, it turned out, were hardliners *against* illegal immigration in any form. Being that they were the only ones able to vote, and sided squarely with the Republicans on the issue, this was perhaps the most devastating blow of all for the Democratic Party.

The result was a significant widening of Republican majorities throughout the country. The Democrats were lurched farther left by the events. Most of their moderates moved over to the Republican Party, and all that remained were the far leftists and progressives. In some states and even some federal races, the candidates ran as socialists and didn't identify with the Democrats any more at all. New York and California were heavily populated with the far left groups, and Illinois remained in Democrat control by title alone, likely only one election cycle away from having a socialist legislature and governor, as flocks of progressives fled the red states for these progressive havens. Big cities, even in the red states, remained Democrat controlled for the most part, but of a more traditional vein.

Austin was the exception. An ultra-progressive city within one of the most conservative states, the rise of the music culture and tech industry drew leftists from California and New York and they fashioned the city after the socialist composition of those states. The current situation for Austin, however was unique. Unlike the three socialist states, Austin was isolated in its political philosophy. It was an island of about one million people floating in a red sea, with no possibility of changing the composition of the state government in the foreseeable future. Austin's policies, even its presence, had actually drawn Texas further right in each election cycle. Within the socialist bubble of Austin, progressives had a narrow view of their circumstances and were overly optimistic at turning Texas into another left-leaning state, like the California of a decade ago. Insulated by a dense population of those with similar views, they were unable to see exactly how isolated they really were within the conservative state.

Ray looked up at the television screen and sighed. *Now here we were.* He contemplated that it was almost negligent to publish this research paper without addressing what was happening right now. Maybe delaying it and providing an analysis of the rebellion, if that is what this could be called, would be prudent. As he thought about it he chuckled. There would be a delay no matter what at this point. He started writing out his experience over the past couple days.

16.

"Alpha 6-2, your status?" the radio chirped. "Alpha 6-2, your location and status?"

Officer Russel tried to look out the window to get a bearing on where he was. He had been able to push the emergency button on his radio when he regained consciousness, but wasn't sure of his exact location. He tried to open the door, but the roof had crushed in enough to prevent it from opening. There was a stabbing pain in his left thigh.

"Alpha 6-2, I have been hit by a bus, I am upside down and not sure of my exact location," he wheezed. He was having difficulty breathing, his ribs were broken and it pained him to speak.

"Alpha 6-2, copy," the dispatcher replied. "Any available Alpha units, Alpha 6-2 in need of assistance on Route 40 west of the city, exact location unknown."

The radio erupted with units responding. "Alpha 6-2, what is your status?"

"I'm 10-4, but I need medical," Russel responded, "and I am stuck in my squad, it's on its roof."

"Medics enroute, Alpha 6-2," came the reply.
Back at the Amarillo headquarters, Sergeant Rutherford stood in the dispatch window as the dispatcher spoke with Officer Russel. He listened intently to the interaction.

"Check the status on Alpha 6-7 and 6-8," he said.

"We have sir, they are not responding," she told him.
Sergeant Rutherford rubbed his temples. It could be that they are out of range of the radios he told himself. He knew that was not true, and feared something terrible had happened to them.

"How many units are headed that way?" he asked.

"Six, so far," the dispatcher replied.

"Send more," he said. "Hell, send everyone."

17.

Jack was looking at the television screen and heard the Austin chief's statement. He looked at his watch, not sure if it really mattered at this point since the time demands from her seemed fluid at best.

"What do you think, Tim?" He asked. "I am almost wondering if we should move with force and arrest that chief right now, defang the snake. You give the order and my troopers will get it done."

Tim leaned back in his chair. The bus convoy bothered him but he wasn't sure why. It was tugging at the edges of his consciousness and he knew he needed to focus on what was going on outside his home and office right now. "Let's see what she does," he said. "I don't know what she thinks she is going to do with that piece of paper."

"My concern," said Jack, "is that she will get the crowd riled up and enlist their assistance in storming the mansion."

"She might," Tim replied, "and we will deal with that if it happens. Let's let her make the first move. The crowd is already riled up, I don't think anything she does will change that one way or the other."

Tim walked over to the window and looked out on the crowd. There was a large gathering, and it was growing by the hour. Maybe Jack was right, waiting might turn into a riot of epic proportions. Overwhelming the crowd now and taking her into custody might send the crowd into disarray, perhaps more easily dispersed without her there acting as some sort of leader any rallying point. Tim was never indecisive, but this was new territory.

"What would your plan be to take Chief Wilshire in preemptively, Jack?" he asked, still looking at the crowd.

18.

Mac and Seth were two hundred yards out from the governor's mansion. They had parked their car, having removed all VIN tags and registration, about 50 yards outside the edge of the gathering crowd and walked over to a 4th floor apartment they had rented weeks ago under a false name and paid for with cash. Black hoodies made them fit in with the roaming rioters, and the rifles drew no attention in their guitar cases. A stable wooden table was set back into the room, the window open but covered with screen making it difficult to see through from outside. The room had been painted flat black, and both the sniper rifle on the table and Seth behind it were virtually invisible to anyone on the outside of the room. Next to him, Mac looked through a spotting scope at the crowd. The view was completely unobstructed, and the mesh screen would have almost no impact on the big magnum's trajectory at this range.

The Hill Country Militia members had all received a text message earlier in the day signaling them to respond to Austin a day early based on the news coverage Mac had been following.
Up for coffee?

No one answered, the signal had been preplanned and the groups moved to Austin independently. Mac and Seth were providing over-watch as far as the rest of them knew, and the rest of the teams were simply to remain close to the governor's mansion as a quick reaction force if violence erupted and the DPS troopers were overwhelmed. All of the teams were positioned toward the rear of the mansion, out of sight of the crowd. Even the troopers had no idea they were there, as was the plan. If nothing happened, the militia would slip back out of Austin without anyone ever knowing they had been there. If something did happen, no one would ever forget they had been there.

"That Austin chief is going to make a move early," Mac said, looming intently through the eyepiece of his spotting scope. Turned up to 40 power, he was able to see her very clearly at this distance, could almost read her lips. He watched her dancing awkwardly with some of the rioters, paper in one hand and megaphone in the other.

"The Left's hypocrisy is without bounds," Seth said, the crosshairs of the scope centered just below Wilshire's nose, following her as she moved clumsily to some beat they could not hear from their hide.

"Are you ready?" Mac asked.

"Sure am."

Mac pulled a cell phone from his pocket and dialed a number, leaving his thumb on the send button.

"Stand by to send it," Mac whispered.

19.

The screaming and gunfire heard over the radio jolted the dispatcher upright and prompted Sgt. Rutherford to run for his squad. His officers were involved in a pitched gun battle. They reported that there were only two buses and they had them stopped right at the edge of the city. Being pinned in by the density of squad cars responding, the windows of the buses had opened and heavy machine-gun fire was cutting down the Amarillo officers, punching through their squad cars and leaving them no place to find cover. The transmission on the radio was brief, and violent. Then silence. The remaining police units were searching for the buses, having no one left to tell them the direction of travel after the initial encounter. Sgt. Rutherford raced to his fallen men and women, rage coursing through his veins.

The buses pulled into the parking lot of a large shopping mall undeterred. There were no more police cars around at the moment, and the presence of two large buses drew attention only as they might be a celebrity road crew of some sort, news of their destructive path being unknown to those seeing the them pull up to the front main entrance, outside the movie theaters. From the first bus, two men in black hoodies emerged and immediately jumped into the second bus. The first bus remained as the second pulled out of the shopping mall and headed east.

Sgt. Rutherford's squad car whined as he pushed the engine to its performance limits. A feeling of helplessness washed over him, then rage, as he listened to the dispatchers repeated attempted to contact the officers. There was no response from any of them. He was less than two miles from their last known location when a massive fireball appeared in the sky in the direction of the mall. Seconds later came a deafening boom as the sound of the explosion arrived at his location. He slammed on his brakes and watched the fireball shrink back on itself and the wall of billowing smoke rise into the sky.

20.

The DPS SWAT commander shook Tim's hand and left the office. Jack looked at Tim and nodded approval.

"This is the right thing, Tim," he said. "This was your initial gut reaction when this started if you remember, it even a better idea now."

"I hope so, Jack," Tim said somberly. There was going to be a battle, and he would be relegated to watching it from his office window.

"They are ready to move, just coordinating with the riot teams now to make sure there's a plan once this kicks off. Snipers are watching from the top of the capitol building," Jack nodded with a glance toward the upper tower. "We will try to make this fast."

"Any other plans I should know about?" Tim asked.

"Yes, separate arrest teams will be arriving at the homes of the mayor and the City Board members, we are arresting all of them," Jack replied.

"Good," Tim said.

His desk phone beeped and his secretary told him that the Governor of California was on the line. The timing for this call could not have been worse, but at least he might be able to take this other concern off of his plate.

"Dante?" he said into the speakerphone, "Leland here."

"Good morning, Governor Leland," came the soft voice of the man on the other line. "What can I do for you?"

"Dante, there was a convoy of buses that left your Guard base in Los Angeles and is now in Texas. Know anything about it?" Tim said, in no mood to dance around the issue with a man he loathed.

"Not a clue, why?"

"A convoy left *your* National Guard base, and you have no idea why, and you wonder why I might want to know?" Tim responded sarcastically. "Find out and call me back, I have things here to deal with." Tim disconnected the call without waiting for a reply.

Dante leaned back in his chair, then called the commander at the Guard base on his cell phone. Emmanuel Rodriguez, known by his friends as Capo, was the base commander and an ally of the governor's. His devotion to communism was generally known around the base, but in the current California Guard, that meant very little to anyone.

"Dante, mi amigo, how are you," he said upon answering.

"Good, Capo, but I have a quick question. Before you answer, keep in mind the things I should know and the things I do not need to know," Dante said. "Our newer friends at the base, are they still there or what is going on with them."

"Our friends are doing good, Dante. That is probably as much as you want to know," Capo replied.

"Ok, but are they still at the base?" Dante pressed, cautiously.

"They, might have left, some time ago," came the reply.

21.

Seth pressed the rifle slightly forward, loading the bipod, and adjusted the bean bag wedged under the buttstock of his rifle, rendering it perfectly steady. He centered the small red dot of the scope, indicating the center of the crosshairs, on the upper lip of Chief Wilshire, just below her nose.

Mac pressed send on the cellphone, counted to two, and whispered "Send it."

The electronic earmuffs lessened the concussion of the big magnum as Seth squeezed the trigger. Almost simultaneous to the rifle's recoil, a massive explosion rocked the area outside the protestors as the car the two men had parked there detonated its stockpile of explosives.

Seth looked in his scope for the Chief as the rifle settled back in, but she had dropped immediately, the round connecting with massive destruction to her head resulting in instantaneous death. The crowd was in chaos, barely noticing the chief's assassination because of the car bomb. One of the DPS snipers did notice however, and relayed to the troopers on the ground that a shot had been fired from an unknown location. The troopers began to engage individual protestors with rifle fire as they ran toward the mansion, unable to tell if they were running from the bomb or attacking, and unwilling to wait to find out. They continued to use restraint, however, and engaged only individual protesters crossing their line, refusing to fire into the crowd indiscriminately.

The team of SWAT officers that had been staging to arrest the chief poured out from the sides of the mansion. Some of the crowd, the more committed communists, had brought their own firearms to the event. Unlike their progressive allies, they had no opposition to guns and saw them as tools in the furtherance of their cause. Sporadic gunfire came from them in multiple areas, directed toward the DPS troopers and the SWAT team. Each instance was met with an almost instant response from the DPS snipers overlooking the crowd, and their deadly precision was consistent. The Austin police officers who did wear their pistols drew them, and met the same fate.

22.

Ray looked to the television screen as the explosion rocked the news camera filming it. He put the laptop down next to him and leaned in toward the screen, turning the volume up with the remote. The screaming blocked out what the reporter was trying to say, she struggled to stand up after being knocked to the ground by the overpressure from the blast.

There appeared to be multiple bodies thrown about the lawn and surrounding street. Ray looked closely at the screen. He saw the uniformed body of a police officer wearing unmistakable red high heel shoes laying on the ground next to a vehicle.

"That's the Austin police chief," he whispered to himself. A part of him wanted to grab his rifle and head back down to Austin. There was a fight happening, and he hated not being a part of it. But this was no longer his job. He had done what he had to earlier, it didn't bother him to do it, but he also wasn't expected to anymore. He moved his glance from the bag where his AK-47 was up to the pictures of his kids.

His mind raced. The kids were safe with their mom. Death had always been a possibility when he was a cop and they were younger, but he had thought that was long past and he had entered a new phase of his life. A phase that meant he could watch his kids grow up and not wonder if he would always be there for them. He looked at the screen, and back to the bag. Adrenaline pumped into his system. He had already been in this fight, now there were good cops in it and he wasn't. Ray started to move back into his seat, ready to let the current crop of DPS troopers fight this battle, when an alert and breaking news banner flashed across the bottom of the screen:

"Explosion rocks Stephenville shopping center...."

Ray grabbed the duffle bag and sprinted for the door, tucking his 1911A1 into his pants on his way out.

23.

Marie and the four kids were at the back end of the Walmart when the explosion outside happened, demolishing the front third of the building. News of the Amarillo explosion had not yet reached her, and probably would not have matter if it had. The air inside the building was smoke and dust. Sunlight filtered in where the front of the building had been blown away, and portions of the roof had collapsed. She was temporarily stunned, but was regaining her senses quickly. She desperately looked the kids over. They were crying, all but the oldest boy, but were not bleeding anywhere. Marie's ears rang slightly from the explosion. She had never heard anything so loud in her life.

"Stay with me, everyone hold hands" she yelled to the kids. Around them there was chaos as people ran for exits or searched for loved ones. Marie moved to the back of the store, found the employee door to the dock and moved that direction. She paused upon entering the dock, and retrieved her pistol from her purse. She racked the slide of the Walther CCP and flicked off the safety.

"Hold on to my belt," she told her youngest, "everyone get in single file and hold onto the belt of the person in front of you."

The children responded without question. They were obedient children, homeschooled by Marie for their entire life thus far. They were scared, but also had complete trust in their mother. Marie moved forward slowly, pistol in a two-handed grip as Ray had taught her. She thought at first that the explosion might have been some sort of earthquake. Now her gut was telling her to be careful, something was not right. Her plan was to get out of the building through the back doors and move on foot around to the front where she had parked her truck, hoping to get out before there was further collapse.

The dock bay doors were open, and the walls and doors that formed a separation between the store and the warehouse area insulated it from the smoke and the debris in the main part of the store, making her visibility much better here. She moved cautiously but quickly toward the bay doors, staying close to the shelving racks on her right side. Two dark figures appeared in the doorway and she stopped. Praying they were policemen or fireman, she was about to scream out to them when she saw the rifles. The black hoodies indicated these were not emergency responders. She pressed herself and the kids close to the shelving units, enveloped in the shadows.

The figures moved into the warehouse, but turned to their right to make their way to the interior of the store. She watched undetected as they passed, and waited until they went through the doors into the store before turning her attention back to the bay doors. Moments later, she heard gunfire from the inside the store. The kids jumped, and her youngest daughter began crying again.

"C'mon, guys," she said, "stay close together and let's go."

Her cellphone buzzed in her pocket. She paused to look at it. The text message was from Ray.

Don't go out, stay home. Bad things. Will call shortly, on my way to you now.

The message made her more concerned and at the same time was a bit relieving. Now she knew for sure this was something evil, probably terrorism. If it were terrorism it was working, she was surely terrified. But she was also comforted that Ray was on his way. God she wished he were here now, this was Ray's world and she knew he would keep them safe. Before trying to call him, she needed to get out of this building. She could call once she got everyone into the car.

24.

Ray had the Highlander going as fast as it would go. He was northbound on 35, weaving in and out of the occasional vehicle in his way. Traffic was light at this time of day. Marie had not responded to the text he sent her before leaving, and he dared not try to call now. All of his attention was on driving. The old police wisdom held here, 'you can't help anyone if you crash on your way there.'

The news on the radio was reporting nonstop on the events unfolding. So far, there had been explosions in Amarillo, Lubbock, Stephenville, and Abilene. Reports of armed men in massive gunfights with the police were being reported in these locations and on the highways leading to them. The news was reporting a convoy of buses to be somehow involved, and that at least in one incident in Amarillo a bus had been used as a bomb. The death toll in the Amarillo was expected to rise over 1,000 as a shopping mall had been decimated, including a movie theater. Police were continuing to battle with bands of armed terrorists in each city where the explosions had occurred, and the terrorists were heavily armed with military grade weapons.

With the state under siege, reporting had drifted from the battle taking place in Austin to the array of explosions further north. Ray was now only interested in what was going on in Stephenville, where Marie and the kids were. It was getting the least coverage at this point, being more remote and less populated than the other cities.

"Breaking news on the explosion in Stephenville," the reporter's voice interrupted his thoughts, "the bus bomb that has destroyed most of the strip mall on 377 a short while ago appears to have been part of a convoy of buses coming from outside of Texas through New Mexico."

Ray pondered this news, still pressing the Highlander to its top end.

"Sources tell KXAN news that there were as many as ten buses and that the explosions have involved what are believed to be as many as five of those. Police in Stephenville are engaged in gunfire with multiple terrorists who are now occupying the remains of a Walmart in the aftermath of the blast. Casualties are considered 'significant' according to a police spokesman."

Ray thought this had all the markings of a terrorist attack so far. Coordinated VBED's, followed up by small arms fire from attacking terrorists. The connection to what was happening in Austin was not something he considered, outside of a general speculation that the world had gone mad.

25.

Tim was watching the events unfold outside his home and office. The explosion a second ago had brought him to the window. The gunfire below was sporadic, not a pitched battle, and he saw the restraint the troopers were using in deploying deadly force. The crowd was dispersing rather quickly, the combination of explosions and watching their comrades be shot dead was more than most of them had signed up for.

Jack hung up his phone and walked up to Tim.

"We have a major problem, Tim," Jack said urgently.

Without looking away from the melee, Tim asked "you mean besides this?"

"Yes, those buses. Apparently they have been blowing up in populated areas of our smaller cities. Teams of armed terrorists are engaged in gun battles with local cops as we speak," Jack spoke faster than normal.

Tim turned to look at him, eyes wide in disbelief but visibly angered. He went to his desk and told his secretary to get the Governor of California on the phone.

"Governor Leland," the soft, pathetic voice on the other end infuriated Tim.

"What happened, you son of a bitch?" Tim barked at him

"Tim, I am sure I don't know what you are talking about, but I looked into those buses and there is no record of having them on our Guard bases," Dante said condescendingly.

"The fucking satellites saw them leave, you asshole!" he yelled into the receiver.

"I will not be talked to in that," he feebly objected before Tim disconnected the phone.

"That son of a bitch knows something, Jack," Tim said looking at him, seething with rage. "Who do we have responding to those cities?"

"The Guard, I hope you don't mind but I had them redirected since we have this pretty much under control here I think," Jack said.

"No, that was a good idea. Your men are taking care of business down there, get those cities everything they need. Helicopters, tanks, whatever. I am not kidding."

"They are all on their way. SWAT commander also informed me that they have the Austin City Board and mayor in custody as we speak," Jack told him, but Tim's mind was in California right now.

"Get Grace and Clark on the line, tell Grace to prepare an order for martial law in all the affected cities and in Austin. I will announce it immediately."

26.

Marie peered out of the bay door cautiously. The alley behind the store was empty save for a few dumpsters and empty pallets. She led her kids to the right down the back of the store, moving quickly but close to the wall. She heard gunfire coming from inside the walls, amplified as she passed some of the rear doors to the building. Some of the gunfire was outside, coming from the front of the building. She paused for a second to listen and think. The gunfire outside was intensifying, some of it fully automatic. There was no point in going around the building to get to her truck, she was parked right in the middle of a warzone from what she could tell. She looked out at the field behind the Walmart, and guided the kids straight out into it at as fast of a run as her littlest girl could keep up with.

A small creek separated the back of the Walmart lot from what looked to be a private ranch. She picked up her daughter and crossed the creek as the other children held on to her and each other. They all scaled over a barbed wire fence and made their way across some open pasture toward a tree line a few hundred yards away. The sound of the gunfire faded with each step, but the frequency did not.

The children were noticeably more relaxed. Distance helped, but also the fact that they were country kids. Horses and chickens and ducks and fields made up their life. While trips to town were fun, they were not in their most comfortable environment, but this pasture was more like home for them. When they made it to the woods, they might as well have been home.

Marie flipped the Walther's safety back on and tucked it in the front of her jeans. She dialed Ray's cellphone and hoped he would answer.

"Are you ok?" he said immediately upon answering.

"Yes, we are all fine, but my God, Ray."

"Are you at home?"

"No, we were at Walmart, something exploded, and then there were terrorists with guns," she was trying to maintain composure, the reality of what had happened was beginning to settle in and the adrenaline was leaving her body now that she had found safety for her and the kids.

"Where are you now?" Ray asked, trying to stay calm.

"We made it to some woods on a ranch behind the Walmart," she said. "Ray, they are still shooting over there, a lot. We can't go to the truck."

"Ok, I am headed your way. I will be in the area in about an hour. Save the battery on your phone for now and I will call you when I get close to figure out where to pick you up."

Marie hung up her phone and put it in her pocket. She started moving deeper into the woods, looking to come out by a roadway on the other side where she could meet Ray without being near the Walmart. The ground was uneven in the woods, not as flat as the pasture they had come through, but the trees were comforting in the concealment they provided. The kids began to chat, laughing a little and even bickering. They were returning to normal and she was glad to see it. Marie knew that they probably did not understand exactly what had happened, and that was for the better at this point. Marie presumed this was a terrorist attack and hopefully it would be over quickly, once the police had taken out the attackers. She could slow down now and make her way through the woods at her own pace.

27.

The President was on the television giving condolences for the loss of life in the Texas cities and stated he was watching the events in Austin carefully. As was his way, he ended by saying, "but I know Texas, they will handle this swiftly."

Tim smiled as he heard that. Texas did not need federal involvement yet, and it seemed unlikely they would. He would never ask either, but might accept it if it were offered should things get really bad. The current state of federal law enforcement probably ensured there would be no offer to assist without a request. An embarrassing scandal involving the FBI in an attempt to affect the outcome of the presidential election six years ago had gutted the agency of its leadership and moved Congress to defund massive portions of their operations. Counterterror responsibilities, where this current incident would have fallen before, were now relegated to the operation of regional fusion centers and operations outside of US borders. Most of the funding they had received had been shifted to the states to bolster their own police forces in the counterterror field, and interstate task forces had largely replaced the Bureau's footprint in that area. The FBI as a national police force was long gone.

Texas was not a part of any interstate terror task force, relying on their own operations through a division of DPS. They had signed agreements to assist New Mexico, Oklahoma, and Louisiana in an emergency, but were largely self-sufficient in their own state. Jack had ordered the Anti-Terror Teams to respond to all affected cities and to Austin shortly after the first reports of the explosions.

Jack had the commander from the 147th Attack Wing of the Texas Air National Guard on the phone and looked up at Tim.

"One of the MQ-9 Reaper drones is tracking two buses southbound on 35 between Waco and Temple," he said.

"Are they from that convoy?"

"Verifying now."

"Is the drone armed?" Tim asked.

"Yes, it is an attack drone."

Upon confirmation, they are clear to take the buses out," he said without hesitation.

28.

Marie and the kids moved slowly but deliberately through the woods. She used the GPS on her phone to navigate toward a road about two miles through the wooded portion of this massive ranch. Looking at her battery life, she remembered Ray's advice to save her battery, took a good look around to set her bearings, and then shut down the GPS. She had a natural sense of direction and was not overly concerned with getting lost out here. The kids walked alongside her now, no need to hang on to each other, but they remained close. Marie kept an eye toward where they were heading, but also monitored the ground for snakes. There were a lot of rattlesnakes in the area, and this was prime territory to stumble on one.

About an hour later, Marie heard a car through the trees and realized they were very close to the road. She brought the group to a stop, staying in the cover of the trees and out of sight of the road. Pulling up her GPS again, Marie sent Ray a text with the coordinates for where she was at. His response said he would be there in fifteen minutes.

Marie pulled a bottle of water from her purse and passed it around to the kids. They each had a couple of peanut butter crackers from a package she found at the bottom of her purse and then sat down to wait for their father to pick them up.

Marie's phone buzzed to alert her to a new text message from Ray a few minutes later telling her he was waiting in the location she indicated by GPS. The family walked out of the woods to the waiting Highlander at the side of the road, Ray ran over to hug the kids, then carried his littlest daughter to the car. A moment later, they were on their way to Marie's house.

"What about the truck?" she asked looking over at him.

"We'll take a look after this dies down," he said, smiling at her.

Ray and Marie rarely got along for very long, but he was glad she was ok and grateful to her for successfully getting his kids out of there.

"What is going on?" she asked, looking out the window at the passing trees.

"I don't know," he said. "There is some kind of rebellion going on in Austin that is out of control, and then these terrorist attacks in multiple cities. Who would have ever thought to bomb Stephenville?"

"I was pretty scared," Marie whispered, not wanting the kid's to hear. She glanced back and was relieved to see they had all fallen fast asleep.

"I don't blame you," Tim smiled. "But you did good."

"It was really bad, Ray," she said, looking out the window. "The explosion was deafening, and then the roof collapsed on the far side of the store. We were on that side not five minutes before, we would have been right under it. All I could think about was getting the kids out of there. There were mothers running around screaming for their kids, it was terrifying, and heartbreaking."

Ray looked over at her, nodded, and then looked back to the road. He knew her well enough to know that Marie was not able to lock things away in compartments in her mind. She was successful at momentarily blocking the panic in order to handle the situation, but he could tell this was going to bother her as the reality of what she had avoided settled in.

"Thank God for that," he said softly.

"Definitely," she nodded, "Thank God."

29.

The Reaper circled to confirm the buses were destroyed after sending its payload into each of them. All that remained were two charred lumps in the highway. It headed back to the base to reload and would then be prepped and ready to head toward Austin if needed.

On the ground, a team of soldiers from the Texas Army National Guard closed on the buses and began looking for intelligence or evidence. They were almost immediately joined by investigators from the DPS Anti-Terror Division. Though mostly destroyed, the remains of some weapons allowed serial numbers to be traced back to their origins. Two M-249 machine guns and a LAWS rocket had enough identifiers remaining to be entered into the database for a search. The search showed all of the weapons had been assigned to the Los Angeles National Guard base.

There appeared to be the remains of at least twelve people, maybe more, among the debris. The bodies were scorched or damaged beyond recognition, and DNA samples would take a while to come back, but eventually their identities would be known. There were no identifying tags on the buses, no registration plates or VIN tags. All of the identifying numbers had been removed.

The team of forensic experts from the Guard and from DPS moved slowly and methodically through the debris. Each wore a small Geiger counter to detect radiation levels in the event there had been nuclear materials or a dirty bomb aboard the buses. The chemical suits were bulky, but provided an added precaution in case of a biological or chemical threat as well. It made the team's movement slow, but they were in no hurry anyway.

A soldier leaned down over one of the bodies after noticing a small white patch amid the mostly charred black background. A business card remained mostly intact and was sticking out of the charred and torn pocket of a dead man's black pants. He reached down carefully and picked it up.

Peering through the lenses on the mask of his chemical suit, he read the front of the card:

Los Angeles Base Commander: Emmanuelle Rodriguez
California National Guard

On the back was a phone number, but several of the digits were unreadable. The soldier placed the card in a paper envelope he was carrying and signaled to the DPS Anti-terror agent next to him by waving his arm. The DPS agent took the card and moved out of the crime scene before removing his protective gear and retrieving his phone from his pocket. He dialed Jack's number.

30.

"Who the fuck is Emmanuelle Rodriguez?" Tim yelled into the speakerphone at Dante.

"Uh, who?" Dante hesitated.

"Your fucking base commander at the LA Guard unit," Tim spit out, "don't play fucking games with me. One of these damn terrorists had his business card in his pocket when we killed him."

"I, uh, I will look into it, and let you know," Dante stuttered back. This was a troubling development for sure. Dante tried to make himself sound helpful. "Also, Governor Leland, I am being told that there might be some other buses heading your way."

"What the hell are you talking about?" Tim said incredulously.

"That's all I can say for now," Dante responded, and this time he hung up the phone.

Tim sat back in his chair, rage coursing through his veins.

"Tim, the crowd has pretty much dispersed down there, but there are a lot of casualties," Jack said, looking from the window.

"Any troopers hurt?" Tim asked.

"None killed, couple minor injuries, but quite a few civilians and Austin police officers are dead, Tim."

"Ok, we will deal with it," Tim said. "What the hell was that thing about other buses? You think that communist knows there is another attack coming?" he continued after explaining what Dante had just told him on the phone.

"I lost an air unit in that attack on Amarillo, but I have the other one up right now and I can send it toward the New Mexico border to look around," Jack said somberly.

"I'm sorry about the air unit, Jack, I didn't know," he said.

"It's ok, we had a lot going on, didn't need to burden you any further."

"Did you know the aircrew personally?" Tim asked.

"Yes, I am always involved in the selection of those teams," Jack nodded," they are an elite group, I knew every one of them well."

Tim put his hand on Jack's should and squeezed slightly. He turned to the phone and dialed up the commander at the 149th Fighter Wing of Air National Guard at the Kelly Field Annex in San Antonio. They spoke quietly for a few minutes as Jack looked out the window, watching his men start to work on the massive crime scene involving the largest officer-involved shooting event in the history of Texas.

31.

As Sergeant Rutherford began approaching the mall, he saw a man in black pants and black hoodie ducking behind the bushes in front of home, looking in the direction of the blast. He stopped the squad car as the man lifted a machine gun and placed the bipod on a bird bath, aiming it in the direction of the mall across the street.

Rutherford put the car in park, unlocked the AR-15 from the roof rack behind his head, charged the bolt and turned on the Eotech sight. Slipping from the driver's seat, he ducked low and shuffled around the rear of the squad. Using the rear taillight to support the rifle, he placed the center dot on the back of the hooded figure and squeezed the trigger. The hooded man screamed and fell as the 5.56 round tore through his right shoulder blew a small hole out the front.

"Stay down!" commanded Rutherford as he ran toward the fallen enemy. "I will kill you if you move."

Reaching the bushes, Rutherford grabbed the wounded man by the ankle and dragged him out into the front lawn before handcuffing the man, who was writhing in pain.

"I need help, you fucking pig, you shot me," the man spit as he spoke.

"I would put a bullet in your brain right now if I didn't want information from you, you piece of shit," Rutherford said. "My beloved Governor Tim Leland has declared martial law because of you assholes, so believe me when I tell you that you will talk to me, and I will not hesitate to end your pathetic life right here if you do anything except exactly as I say."

Rutherford pulled out a packet of Quikclot and two gauze pads, tearing the packet open with his teeth before pouring the coagulating granules into both the entrance and exit wounds and packing them with the gauze. The hemostatic granules did their job, but burned in the process causing the man to yelp and curse. After wrapping the gauze tightly on the front and back holes in the man's shoulder, Rutherford jerked the man off the ground by his other arm and walked him to his squad before unceremoniously tossing him into the back seat. He returned to retrieve the M-249 machine gun from the front lawn where it had fallen off the birdbath and put it in the rear of his cruiser.

"I have one in custody, Alpha 6-0," he said into his radio.

"10-4, Alpha 6-0 has one in custody," the dispatcher responded.

"Status at the explosion site?" he asked.

"We have multiple EMS teams and Guard units on scene. All off-duty units have been notified to report immediately," she responded.

"10-4, I am heading back to the station with mine," he advised.

The shift lieutenant had arrived at the mall and would supervise the efforts there. A Guard colonel was awaiting his prisoner at Amarillo PD, and information extraction would begin shortly.

"Have an EMS unit meet me at the station, dispatch," Rutherford said.

"10-4, nature of the injuries?" she asked in order to relay to EMS.

"Gunshot wound."

32.

Waiting in the command center set up at the Amarillo police station, Major James Thompson paced slowly across the floor. He was a young man for his rank having been in the Texas Army National Guard since the day he was eligible to join. A graduate of Texas A&M, he was smart and fit. His troops adored him, as did most people he met. He had done tours in both Gulf Wars, three in the current campaign. As an intel officer, he was anxious to get his hands on the prisoner the Amarillo sergeant was bringing in, perhaps literally.

A staff sergeant came into the board room where Jack was pacing him and handed him a cup of hot coffee. James took it with a smile and went back to pacing. The Amarillo police radio sitting on the board room desk let him know what was going on from their end on the ground and helped him coordinate his Guard units to supplement their efforts. Most of them were deployed at the mall helping evacuate casualties, and clearing the rubble. Rutherford's last transmission let him know the suspect being brought in had probably already been shot. That could be good or bad depending on how bad he was hit.

Rutherford reported over the radio that he was at the station and James sent his staff sergeant to help Rutherford bring him in. He put plastic sheeting on office chair, no need to ruin a good chair, and moved it against the wall in the corner of the room. He brought a five gallon water bottle over along with a towel that he placed on the table. Three sets of handcuffs were also on the table.

As Rutherford and the staff sergeant dragged the suspect into the room, James directed them to put him in the chair. The suspect was cursing and winced each time he was moved. With the hoodie down, the parts of his matted blonde hair that were not soaked in sweat fell in front of his eyes. James looked at him and thought he looked like some kid who should be skateboarding in a parking lot. This enemy was vastly different than the Taliban suspects he had done this dance with previously. The fight in his eyes was mostly faked. The commitment would flee as pain and fear entered the picture. There would be no welcoming of death here, no promise of 72 virgins awaiting his departure from this world. This enemy was soft and weak.

Rutherford and the staff sergeant un-handcuffed one hand, sat him in the plastic covered office chair, and cuffed him to the arm rest. The staff sergeant then retrieved the other three sets of handcuffs and secured the suspect's free hand and both ankles to the chair. The EMS unit arrived and quickly changed the dressing Rutherford had applied to the wound, having been advised already that this would not be a full-service treatment. As the EMS attendant left, James walked over to the suspect.

The look in the suspect's eyes was changing slowly from anger to fear. As the pain from his shoulder started to lose some of its edge, it was harder to subdue the fear driven by the searing pain of the initial injury.

"What's your name, son," James asked him softly.

"Fuck you is my name," came the response. "I am not your son."

James grabbed the back of the chair and slammed it forward, smashing the suspect's face into the floor. He pressed the back of the chair into the back of his neck and leaned on it.

"Ok, ok, ok, please let me up," he whimpered.

"What's your name, *son*?" Jack asked again softly.

"Adam, my name is Adam," he gasped. "Adam Dansforth. You're breaking my neck!"

James lifted the chair off his neck, and with assistance from the Rutherford and the staff sergeant he placed the chair and Adam back in an upright position. Pain was still coursing through Adams body, but fear was now the primary emotion he felt.

"Adam," James started softly, squatting down in front of him to look him in the eyes, "you are going to answer every question I ask you today, right?"

Adam's eyes were wide and his breathing heavy, but he didn't say anything.

"Adam, you know I will only ask you one time and then there will be pain, ok?" James said softly.

Adam nodded his head slowly after hesitating, and cast his eyes to the floor. James looked at him and read his body language. This was someone with some training, maybe even military training, but not much experience and even less heart. He would be easy to break.

"Are you a Muslim, Adam?" James asked.

"No, I have no religion, all of that shit is made up to keep the masses down," Adam said, trying hard to sound defiant but already having decided, on some level, that answering this man's questions was not optional.

"Are you a part of any terrorist organization?" James asked.

"No, I am part of the new chapter though. I am a patriot sent to destroy the Nazis and bigots and purge them from our country," Adam said.

"See, we are doing good, you and I, aren't we?" James said softly. "We are going to get along just fine."

Adam looked at him a little confused. He expected a retaliatory action from his captors for calling them Nazis and bigots, but they seemed unmoved.

"Adam, who are you with specifically? Who sent you to Texas?" James asked.

Adam hesitated. James looked at him, tilted his head slightly and frowned. In a lighting fast action, James pulled an ASP collapsible baton from his belt and in one swift motion flicked it open and then arched it forward, smashing it across the knuckles of Adam's left hand as he gripped the armrest of the chair. Adam screamed in pain, doubling forward, resting his head on his broken hand and sobbing.

"Adam, who are you with specifically? Who sent you to Texas?" came the question in the same tone and manner.

"I told you, I am part of a new chapter," Adam sobbed without lifting his head. "We have cells all over, we have no name."

"Are you a member of the Resistance?" James asked.

"We don't call ourselves that," Adam said slowly, "that's what you people call us."

"That's understandable," James nodded, "we don't call ourselves Nazis and bigots, so your point is well taken."

"That's what you are, though, right?" Adam looked up at James. "Admit it!" his voice attempting to achieve something of a defiant tone.

James moved his face close to Adam's, looking him straight in the eye. "I will ask the questions here, understand?" he said softly. "Are you a member of the California National Guard, Adam?"

Adam looked up at him, his hand swelling quickly. "No, why would you ask that?"

"Did your convoy of buses leave the Los Angeles National Guard base, Adam?" James asked him.

"How did you know that?" Adam looked surprised.

"There you go again, Adam," James said shaking his head. "You are asking questions again."

Adam had given up resistance, he had no fight left in him and assumed that James knew everything he was going to tell him already anyway. He had no interest in finding out what other ways James would cause him pain if he resisted. Adam explained in detail how Capo had recruited him during street protests in the aftermath of the last presidential election. How he had been homeless but Capo let him live on the base in LA, along with a few dozen others like him. Capo had trained them with firearms and told them they were chosen for a special mission, that even the Governor would be proud of them if they succeeded. He laid out in detail what that mission was, how the targets were chosen, how the explosives were arranged in the buses. James listened as long as Adam spoke, letting him speak uninterrupted.

Rutherford held his rage. He desperately wanted to avenge his men and his community, and a part of him regretted not killing this useless human where he found him, despite the wealth of information he was now giving them. When Adam finally stopped speaking, he looked at his captors with some relief. He had almost nothing else to tell and felt he would be rewarded for cooperating with them.

"Who is Capo, exactly?" James asked.

"Emmanuel Rodriguez is his real name, he runs the base there," Adam said.

James looked at his sergeant and then at Rutherford. "Would you guys mind getting EMS in here to give him another look over, maybe some pain meds? Let's put him in a cell for now." Adam leaned his head forward to rest on his broken hand and sobbed, this time from relief.

33.

Mac sent out a text message to his militia group.

Sorry, can't make it for coffee today

This was the stand down order that had been prearranged now that the Austin incident was wrapping up. There would surely be more disorder in the coming days, but the crowds were dispersed for now and there was no threat from the Austin police force left to speak of. None of the other members knew about the shot Seth had taken, and none of the other members had engaged during the fighting because the DPS troopers never looked like they were going to be overwhelmed. It had been a successful operation to be sure, but only Seth and Mac knew the extent of that success.

Seth was putting his rifle back into the bag and both men checked the apartment for anything they might have missed before leaving. This would be the last time they would come to this place and wanted no evidence that they were ever hear.

Mac received a text message on his phone.

Emmanuel Rodriguez. Capo. Base commander. LA National Guard.

He glanced at Seth and showed him the message. He then selected six of the militia members from his squad and sent them another group text.

Let's grab a snack at my place.

Seth and Mac walked out of the apartment ten minutes later and into a waiting Chevrolet Suburban with six tough men waiting inside. They threw their gear in back and climbed in.

"We have a new mission, boys, if you're up for it," Mac said as the Suburban cruised toward the highway. Without hesitating they all nodded and muttered agreement. As a group, they had been itching to get into the fight and that itch was far from being sufficiently scratched by today's anticlimactic withdrawal.

Mac's team of eight in the Suburban represented the founding membership of the Hill Country Militia Group Section Alpha. They had all trained together since the beginning, most of them had served overseas. Seth and two others were strictly former law enforcement, but the remaining were former military. Every branch was represented, but every man was a native Texan. The Suburban moved along steadily with no indication of the deadly nature of its passengers.

"We were hit up north, hard. Multiple cities, multiple bombs, lot's of casualties. A lot of them were cops," he began. "We have an opportunity to hit back. We will need to go to California, though, land of fruits and nuts."

The driver glanced back, "when can we leave?"

"Tomorrow morning," Mac said, laughing at the driver's enthusiasm. "Bring all your gear, meet at my place at 0500 hours. We will caravan in two cars, four per vehicle. I know you didn't get to get into the fight tonight, boys, but I promise you that this next mission will get you into the fight." Mac looked at Seth and smiled, patting him on the shoulder. Seth smiled back and leaned his head back on the headrest. He was asleep in a few short minutes.

34.

Ray pulled into the gravel driveway leading up to Marie's house. The horses looked up from eating their hay to see who was here. As they pulled up to the house, Ray looked back to see all the kids still sleeping in the back seats.

"You want to stay over tonight?" Marie asked. Normally Ray went home after visiting the kids every other weekend, rarely staying at the house unless she needed him to housesit while she went out of town with the kids.

"Sure, I can do that," Ray replied. He was glad she offered, he really wanted to be near the kids while this was going on and now that the attack had happened so close to home for them he felt the need to be there to protect them. Something in Marie's voice told him she needed him to be here now too, not out of any rediscovered affection for one another but rather for security.

Having run out of the house so fast, Ray did not have a change of clothes or anything else. As he gently woke up the kids and they walked into the house, he realized that the only things he had brought were his guns, ammunition, and a first aid kit. He quickly became unconcerned as he remembered that Marie was somewhat of a prepper. Actually, she was more of a hoarder, he thought, but prepper was more polite. There was no shortage of food or anything else in the house.

"You think it was Muslims?" Marie asked.

"Might be, still don't know if it could be related to the thing in Austin," he said looking at her. "Not the same thing, though. This looked more like terrorism and the Austin thing was a protest or riot kind of. My issue with the connection is the timing. That can't be coincidental."

"Thanks for coming to get us," Marie smiled at him. "I am going to go take a shower and get dinner ready for the kids. You want anything to eat?"

"No thanks, I need to sit down for a bit," he said, suddenly realizing how tired he had was. He watched Marie walk to her room, remembering again how pretty she was. He momentarily wished they could have gotten along better. He shook his head and reminded himself that the bad times had far outnumbered the good during their tumultuous marriage. Maybe not in the beginning, but for the last few years for sure.

Ray turned on the news in the kitchen, letting the kids watch their cartoons in the living room. The coverage was nonstop between the cities that had been hit and the events in Austin. Reports of casualties were staggering. The blasts had targeted highly populated events, such as the theater in Amarillo and the Wal-Mart in Stephenville. Some of the survivors of the initial blast wer cut down by small arms fire in the follow-up attacks. There were still a few gunfights erupting between the police and the terrorists in a couple of the cities, though most reports showed the police eliminating threats efficiently in each city they were engaged.

The news reported that at least one subject had been taken into custody, but didn't say where. Video footage from the Reaper drone showed the preemptive strike on the buses. The ensuing wreckage had slowed down Ray's trip up to Stephenville by briefly shutting down 35, but he had cut through backroads to make his way to Marie and the kids. The destruction shown by the drone strike was massive, and a secondary explosion in the front bus indicated it was probably rigged to be a bomb for another city.

Ray's cellphone rang, the number indicated it was from Austin. He answered it on the third ring, not sure who it might be.

"This is Ray," he said.

"Ray, it's Clark Bentley, how are you?" the lieutenant governor asked. Ray had gotten to know Clark a little while working closely with him and his staff on a few bills during the last legislative session. Ray found him immediately likeable, and more knowledgeable on a variety of policy issues than any politician he had ever met. In most political offices, the staff are the policy experts and drive the focus of the office holder. This was not true in Clark's office, where his staff more often than not used him as a resource for their policy work. Clark and Ray got along well, and the lieutenant governor would occasionally call to ask him a policy question.

"I'm fine sir, how are you?" Ray said.

"Been better, to be honest," Clark chuckled. "Ray, I wanted to see if we could use you for some policy advice in the next few days. Grace and I are relocating temporarily up near Waco at the DPS offices, are you able to come to our office there tomorrow at some time?"

"Yes, of course I can. I won't be going back down to Austin any time soon either, sir," Ray said. "Is noon ok for you?"

"That's perfect, we'll see you then," Clark said. "I will text you the address in the morning."

Ray looked at the phone and wondered what policy issue they could possibly be working on under the current circumstance that might require his advice. While most of Ray's policy work revolved around policing, he was currently focused on the political science aspect of the nation's politics and hadn't been working on policing or homeland security issues for some time. He supposed he would find out soon enough what they thought he could be of assistance with.

Ray went into the living room and sat next to Sarah, the youngest. She looked at him with a smile on her face, her chocolate brown eyes were soft and full of life. He reached over and ruffled Jason's hair, before playfully pushing him into his oldest son, Matt. The second oldest, Dina was also the most mature. She smiled at them and knew this was the start of a wrestling match, which it soon turned into. She piled on top as everyone wriggled and giggled on the sofa, Sarah screaming out in laughter.

Marie came out from her room in jeans and t-shirt, her hair wrapped up in a towel. "What are you nuts doing out here?" she said laughing.

Ray glanced up at her from the middle of the pile of twisting and laughing bodies and said, "Therapy, for them and me."

35.

The phone on Tim's desk beeped and he heard his secretary's voice.

"Governor, I have a Mr. Miguel Torrez on the line, he says he is with the Department of Interior in Mexico."

"Tim Leland here," he said into the speakerphone after hearing the phone make the transfer connection.

"Governor Leland, thank you for taking my call," the voice on the other end said, only the slightest Spanish accent audible in his English.

"Yes, sir, what can I do for you," Tim said as a courtesy. He was eager to get off the line and get back to the problems at hand.

"Mr. Leland," the man said, "I am going to talk for a few minutes and then get off the line. I will not be able to take any questions, ok?"

"Sure, I suppose," Tim replied.

"Mr. Leland, first, I am sorry for the pain the people of your state have suffered today. One month ago, a Mr. Dante Malone, I am sure you have heard of him, came to Mexico for a conference. While he was here, he spoke with some people, their identities would surprise him if he knew who they really were," the man spoke slowly and clearly.

"He asked them questions about recruiting. He explained that he was inspired by the effectiveness of the drug cartels that had been able to recruit Mexican Special Forces into their ranks," the voice paused for a moment. "This was particularly interesting for the people he was discussing this with, but then his topic changed to another. It was not narcotics he wished to discuss. He wanted to know if they thought such a model could be used to run an insurgency, or terrorist operation. Those were his words."

Tim started to ask a question, then thought better of it. He grabbed a pen and pad and began taking notes. He signaled to Jack to come over and record the call.

"Too much tequila for Mr. Dante apparently that evening. He told the people of his inquiry that he was hoping to rid America of its racist culture. He said that the center of that culture was in Texas, and that if Texas collapsed, the country would easily fall into a socialist philosophy that would be friendlier to Mexico," the man paused for a moment again.

"Mexico has no interest in a conflict with the United States, Mr. Leland, even the recent trade disputes are of little consequence to the overall benefits of our friendship with America. Contrary to Mr. Dante's ill-informed ideas, even the cartels are not interested in such a war with America, bad for business there too you know? Mr. Dante hinted at his access to supplies and his control over the state's military. I am not informed enough to tell you there is a connection between this conversation and today's attacks in your cities, but you should have this information," the man said.

"I know you said no questions, but I have many. Would you entertain two or three, answer only the ones you want to?" Tim asked hopefully.

"You may ask, I will decide to answer or not," the man said.

"Was Dante able to recruit Mexican Special Forces, is that what we are looking at?" Tim asked.

"No, the people he spoke to were not of the sort to relay such a request," the voice said.

"Only other question I have then is why you called me instead of the FBI or CIA?" Tim asked.

"Mexico and Texas have a……special history, Mr. Leland, do we not?" the man chuckled.

"Yes, we sure do," Tim said.

"That is all I can help you with, Mr. Leland. God be with you," the man said and disconnected.

Tim disconnected the phone and leaned back in his seat. He looked over at Jack.

"Do you believe this?" he said incredulously.

"You think this guy was legit?" Jack asked.

"What he said makes me think that somehow Dante ended up talking to some undercover narcotics guys in Mexico who initially thought he was going to be involved with the cartels but then he shifted to the insurrection topic," Tim said.

"That's what I got out of it as well," Jack nodded.

"So the guy calling is either from a Mexican federal narcotics team or he is from their intelligences services would be my guess," Tim said. "He is right about our special history, but my guess is that while Mexico does not want a fight with America, Mexico also doesn't mind when America fights with itself, hence calling me instead of the President or the feds."

"Do you think he is just fanning the flame?" Jack asked.

"I don't know, the bus convoy originating from the California Guard base is not publicly known yet," Tim reminded Jack. "My first guess during a terrorist attack would not have been that California was behind it. Hell, it wouldn't be in my top fifty guesses. I don't think it would be anyone's guess. So the timing can't be coincidental."

"Good point," Jack said.

The reality that Dante Malone might have had some hand in coordinating this attack caused blood to rush to Tim's face. He was mad enough when he suspected it might be Dante's incompetence that let it originate from his state. The idea that it might have been a deliberate attack that Dante had a part in orchestrating was almost too much to consider.

"How could he possibly think he could keep this from being discovered, Tim?" Jack asked. "There is no way he could be so naïve."

"You heard that guy on the phone, he is out actively soliciting for operators. He doesn't seem to care if it is found out," Tim said. "Or he is just that stupid. I am open to either theory to be honest."

36.

Ray pulled into the parking lot of the DPS station just before noon the next day. The news was still wall to wall coverage of yesterday's events, but there was nothing else happening currently. As he walked into the front lobby, he saw a trooper with an M-4 rifle standing guard. He nodded at the trooper and went to the receptionist behind the bulletproof glass.

"Ray Tucker, here to meet with Clark Bentley," he said to her.

"Oh, yes Mr. Tucker. We've been expecting you," she said with a smile in her heavy south-Texas accent. "I will buzz you in, first door on your right."

Tim walked into the room and Clark met him immediately. He reached out to shake his hand.

"Thank you for coming, Ray," he said. "Let's go into the conference room, Grace is there too."

Ray followed Clark into the conference room. There were no windows, but very good lighting. A large mahogany table surrounded by eighteen chairs filled most of the room. A whiteboard and a large computer screen completed the contents. A woman on the far side stood up and walked around the table to shake his hand.

"Grace Headey," she said, extending her hand.

"Ray Tucker," he responded, taking her hand momentarily. Ray had seen Grace on television, and had spoken to her staff a few times by telephone, but he was momentarily taken by how beautiful she was in person. He long red hair was pulled back and tied up, complementing the chiseled features of her face.

They all took seats at one end of the table, Clark at the head of the table and Grace and Ray across from each other.

"Ray," Clark began, "you've done some work on secession in the past for the Liberty Policy Foundation, haven't you?"

"I, uh, yes, a few years ago we put out a paper analyzing the politics and processes that a secession might entail," Ray answered, a little surprised by the topic. "It was in response to something the former governor had said and had become a hot topic here in Texas."

"Yes, I remember that clearly," Grace said smiling, "that caused quite a buzz."

"Ray, you are a former cop right?" Clark asked.

"Yes, sir, retired from Illinois," Ray said.

"What brought you to Texas?" Clark asked.

"Weather, and the ex-wife. She was coming here with or without me, so I came with her," he said.

"Can we swear you to secrecy, Ray?" Grace asked him.

"Of course, as a matter of practice the Foundation does not openly discuss anything we work on with elected officials, ever," he replied sincerely.

"Yes, I know your Foundation is excellent at that, but I mean even your team at the Foundation," she said. "You cannot discuss this with anyone."

"No problem at all," Ray replied, smiling at her.

"Ray, would you be able to come here for the next few days, maybe longer, and act as a consultant to Grace and I?" Clark asked. "I assume you won't be going down to Austin anytime soon."

"Sure, I will let my boss know that I am going to work remotely for a while, pretty sure everyone will be," Ray answered. "Our building was damaged during the initial rioting."

"Good, we would like you to work on the secession topic with us," Clark began. "Let me correct that. Good that you will be working with us, not that your building was damaged," he smiled politely. "We are primarily interested in what a completely sovereign state government might look like and the broader coalition of the other states. Not as part of a war, but of a peaceful separation."

Ray looked at him with interest. The topic had been fun to work on when he did it, but had not been considered with any seriousness since the election of the current president. There were less states' rights issues now, and the current man in the White House was a true believer in small government federalism. Secession was not on anyone's mind anymore.

"Yes, I would be happy to, sir." Ray said. "Is this something we are looking at seriously again? I thought the change in federal policies had rendered little interest in that anymore."

"You're right, there is not much interest in secession anymore," Grace said. "We are interested in where you will arrive at, what policy proposals you would recommend should there be a dispute between two or more states combined with a federal government that is completely neutral or refuses to involve itself. It seems that post-secession that would be something to consider, but you didn't go that far in your previous research. We are asking you to do that now."

"I think I follow what you're asking for, and maybe I don't need to know this information, but why would you want that if there will be no secession?" Ray asked.

"That's a fair question," Clark said. "We think the policy proposals you will arrive at might have applications in the current political environment. This President is noninterventionist when it comes to the states. If a dispute, even a really bad one, happened between two or more states, we are not sure the feds would be involved in resolving it."

"That's a good observation," Ray said. "Yes, I would be happy to help."

"Great, you can share my office with me and start tomorrow," Grace said.

Ray smiled at her and stood to leave. Working in an office with Grace was certainly far from the worst thing he could be doing while waiting to be able to return to Austin.

"We are briefing the governor in a few minutes, Ray," Clark said. "After tomorrow, you will be in on those calls, we want to give him a heads-up first though."

"That is no problem at all, sir, I look forward to the opportunity to work with all of you," Ray said.

"You're in Texas, Ray. It's 'y'all,' not all of you," Grace said chidingly.

"I know," Ray laughed, "but I am still from Illinois where 'y'all' is not a real word."

Ray stood to shake their hands again and then let himself back out into the lobby. He felt like he had a job to do now, something related to the events that were happening, and it seemed to ground him a little.

As he drove back toward his house, he thought about the research he was being asked to conduct or at least to consult on. A conflict between the states seemed and odd topic given what just happened and everything that was going on in Austin. Maybe they were considering in that light given that Austin was claiming its own sovereignty, like a state. He supposed he would learn more tomorrow when he officially started working and would be read into the operations more thoroughly.

37.

The eight members of the Hill Country Militia Group arrived before dawn in Marble Falls and met in the same barn they had been in just a few days ago. Things were different now. No more wondering what would happen, no more speculation of anticipation. First blood had been drawn, and they were pretty sure now who had drawn it. Some rogue commander with the California National Guard was now their target, and only these twelve knew that fact or even knew there would be an operation under way.

They would take two cars, four men per vehicle, rented under false names. The groups would leave a half hour apart, taking different routes, and meet at a prearranged set of hotels just outside Los Angeles County where they would establish a temporary basecamp. All of the men had their weapons and ammunition in bags in the back of the rented SUV's, but they would wear jeans and t-shirts and other casual attire for the trip. No hats or other items with insignia or lettering or anything that someone might remember or identify them by. All of their weapons were legal, and each had a concealed carry permit for their pistols. If confronted by law enforcement, they would be fully cooperative as they were not currently engaged in anything illegal.

The two teams shook hands and the first car headed west just before 6am. The remaining team went to a local cafe to grab some food before departing at the allotted interval. Mac and Seth chatted with their teammates. Joe Spencer was a former cop, and he and Seth talked cop shop while devouring a pile of pancakes and bacon. David Pagan was a former Army Special Forces operator. He knew Mac from the service, but had not been on deployments with him, spending much of his operational career in northern Africa. The four of them were a formidable group, and the full eight man team was a real force to be reckoned with.

Mac was in good spirits. He was completely at ease with both the mission and the men he was with. Outside of the military, Mac had not been very interested in relationships with people until staring this militia group. He found that civilian life offered very little in the way of loyalty and patriotism, that most people he encountered were too wrapped up in their own affairs to be bothered with being a part of something bigger. He didn't dislike them for it, not at all. It actually made him proud to know that his service, and the men sitting here with him and others like them, made that kind of life possible for them. He was proud that they could live a life without fear, that the hardest decision many of them would make today was where they would eat lunch. God bless them in their innocence. He just found that he had little in common with people like that.

When their time came to depart, Seth jumped in the driver's seat as the others settled in to try to sleep. They would rotate drivers and make the trip in one straight shot, no stopping except for fuel and restrooms. The sun was just starting to appear over the Texas hills when they left, Seth looked at the beauty of the hill country one last time and then headed west.

38.

Ray arrived for his first official day of consulting at the Waco DPS office and was given a key card to access the secure area of the building. A trooper led him to the office he would be sharing with the Attorney General for at least the next few days. Grace was not there yet, and Ray set up his laptop on the round conference table in the back area of the office, leaving the actual desk to Grace and a little bit of room for privacy.

As he checked his emails, he noticed that Dave had announced the downtown office for the Foundation temporarily closed. His instructions were to work from home until otherwise advised. Ray sent him an email to update him on what he was doing with the lieutenant governor and Grace. Dave replied that he was ecstatic about this interaction, and would be relaying it to the Foundation's board immediately. Ray did not disclose the nature of his involvement with them, and Dave knew better than to ask at this point.

Grace walked into the office with two cups of coffee in her hand, bringing one to Ray and handing it to him with a smile that made her face even more beautiful. Ray thanked her and offered her a seat at the table by him, which she accepted.

"Ray," she began, "we are interested particularly in how one state might use force against another." She paused to study his reaction.

"Well, ma'am," he started after inhaling deeply.

"Call me Grace, please."

"Well, Grace, I am not an attorney, I should start with that," he said.

"I know, Ray, I am an attorney," she smiled at him. "I am not looking for a legal justification or something found in Constitutional law. I am interested in the political analysis surrounding it. Sort of a prediction of responses by the federal government and or the other states."

Ray leaned back in his chair. "Do you think that another state, an American state did this?" he asked incredulously.

"I can't answer that directly, Ray, but why don't you use that for your starting point in your analysis. What would a response, by force, precipitate? What should be the objective of a response by force? Punitive? Retributive? Compensatory? Consider all of the options you can think of," she guided.

Ray was stunned. This was not a terrorist attack then. At least not in the vein of terrorism that had been this country's priority in combating. This was an attack by another state, a member of the *United* States of America. His held swirled.

"Also consider messaging," she continued, "we have seen your policy work and how you have framed the issues to maximize support for your preferred positions. How might the governor's office message this or should we message it at all? What I mean is, is there an option for covert action and what are the dangers of that, politically?"

"I can do that. Should I give you a few thoughts to see if we are on the right path?" he asked.

"Sure," she smiled at him, her gaze threatening to derail his thoughts.

"Well, initially, I don't think we would want to message it at all until after the retaliation takes place," he began. "I use the word, retaliation, because I think most Texans would want that. But there should also be a preventative reason, force should be used to prevent another attack. There will be an immediate, visceral reaction from each political ideological tribe. Broadcasting that beforehand runs the risk of changing both the effectiveness of the operation or operations as well as interference from the federal government or other parties. Can I ask what state this might be, hypothetically?"

"California, hypothetically," she responded after a moment's pause.

"Ok, well, there would be the obvious optics of conservative Texas and socialist California," he continued. "The other states would fall into one or the other camp for the most part, but many of them would not take a side at all, considering it to be 'not their problem'. Even within the states there would be supporting and opposing views."

"That is one of our concerns, how do you see Texans reacting internally?" Grace asked eagerly.

"I think Texans will be outraged to find out that Californians attacked them, I think they would demand retaliation if they knew," he said. "Outside of Austin, which is probably mostly in shambles now, there would be overwhelming support for any sort of retaliation, a more disliked state than California would be hard to think of in Texas."

"So you think the public would support the use of force to retaliate?" she asked.

"Absolutely," Ray answered without hesitation. "In full disclosure, Grace, my ex-wife and our kids were in that Walmart that got hit in Stephenville, so if I am biased at all it would be for that reason alone. I want to hit them back, hard. Bias aside, I think most Texans would if they knew."

Grace's eyes opened wide upon hearing that. "Are they ok," she asked hesitantly, "your family?"

"Oh, yes, they are all fine, but they could just as easily have not been so fine," he said, tapping the table with his trigger finger. He didn't feel the need to tell her about the shooting he had been in, he had already compartmentalized it and quite frankly hadn't thought about since the explosion in Stephenville had shifted his attention to his family's safety.

"If this was California," he said slowly, "I would want retaliation. There were a lot of people killed that day, their families will want retaliation."

"What are your initial thoughts then?" Grace asked.

"Make the case, just like you would in court, Grace," he said with a smile. "Prove to the public that it was California and your messaging battle is already won."

39.

On an open stretch of US40 about fifty miles west of Albuquerque, the smoldering remains of three buses blocked all eastbound traffic. An MQ-9 Reaper circled briefly as video and photos were taken of the aftermath of its successful attack before heading back east to return to Ellington. A DPS helicopter was on its way to the scene with a team of forensics experts from DPS on board, the governor of New Mexico having given permission to Tim for his people to conduct the forensics exam. She had not been happy about the strike occurring in her state without any warning, but Tim had assured her that the urgency of the situation didn't allow it, reminding her that the buses were just outside Albuquerque when they were destroyed and their destination was unknown. For all anyone knew, it could have been Albuquerque that was the target this time.

"I think the New Mexico governor is a sharp lady, Jack," Tim said after getting off the phone with her. "She is going to put this together pretty quickly would be my guess."

"Probably, but she is allowing us to run the investigation which tells me she doesn't really want any part of it," Jack said.

"I agree, but I am going to try not to surprise her anymore either," Tim nodded. "We might need her at some point and I don't want to burn that bridge."

"I want that DNA analysis on the bodies done as soon as possible. We need to know if those terrorists were members of the California Guard," Tim paused, "I'm not sure if would make any difference at this point or how much of a difference, but I want to know."

"The state crime lab has samples and is actively working on it. The only way we are going to get something is if their DNA were already put into the NDIS system for some reason previously, so don't depend on the idea of identifying them this way too heavily, Tim," Jack cautioned. "I don't want you to get your hopes up. The guy in custody in Amarillo will be valuable, he is talking."

40.

Adam looked up from the cot in his cell as the door unlocked electronically and James slid it open with a loud metallic clunk. He was cradling his wrapped hand and had a pathetic look of self-pity on his face. James casually walked into the cell and toward Adam. He swiftly grabbed the forelock of Adam's hair, yanking him forward off the bed and smashing his fist into the base of Adam's jaw, sending Adam crashing to the ground with a thud. He then stomped on Adam's bandaged hand, causing a guttural scream to come from him that had equal parts fear and pain.

"I expected more from you, Adam," James said calmly.

"What? I told you what you wanted to know," Adam sobbed. "What do you want?"

"The other buses, the three we just blew up in New Mexico, why did you leave that out?" James asked.

"I don't know anything about three other buses", he sobbed. "I told you, we have different cells and we don't know anything about each other."

"Ok, I want to believe you, but answer this," James said, helping Adam back onto his cot, "Are all of you, these unnamed separate cells, are all of you in California?"

Adam looked up at him, fear in his eyes.

"Don't make me hurt you again, Adam," James said calmly, "there are no rules here anymore."

"California is the rally point, all of the cells are there at some point or start from there," Adam confessed. "I don't know where or how many, but we all go to California initially."

"Is Emmanuelle Rodriguez the central point of contact?" James asked.

"No, he is the base commander in LA, and he gave us some training, but I don't think he runs the outfit," Adam said, wincing in pain and holding his hand again. The gunshot wound in his shoulder had stopped bleeding and a local anesthetic meant that his hand actually hurt worse now than his shoulder did.

"Who runs the outfit?" James asked.

"I don't know, honestly, I don't know," Adam said, still clutching his smashed hand and working his jaw trying to tell if it was broken.

"Adam, I am going to ask you if you are aware of any other operations. If you are, you should tell me now," James whispered to him. "Adam, if there is another attack that you failed to tell me about, and we capture someone else to extract information from, I am going to kill you. Do you understand? Your value right now is that you are the only stupid bastard we caught and haven't killed yet."

"I, I, ok I remember hearing something about another possible operation coming after ours," Adam stuttered. "It was supposed to be a few weeks later, meant to crush the morale in Texas as they just started to rebuild from the initial attack, the same cities."

"Same kind of attack?" James asked.

"I don't think so," Adam said, "I think this one had something to do with biological weapons…I remember them talking about UCLA."

"Do you know anything about Austin, what was going on there?" James asked.

"There were supposed to be two buses going to Austin, to the capitol building," Adam said. "We were a little ahead of schedule to be honest. I think there was a reason we were supposed to arrive a day later but I don't remember what it was, my area was Amarillo."

"Could it have been the arrival of the state legislature?" James asked.

"Yes, yes, that's it," Adam said nodding agreement.

"Was the plan to blow up the Capitol?" James asked.

"That, and the Governor's mansion, I think," Adam said nodding.

41.

"What's left of the Austin police department?" Tim asked, looking at Jack.

"I think they are out of commission, a few were killed yesterday during the attack, the rest ran. Our SWAT team has seized the headquarters building, none have returned so far."

"You don't think they will be a problem?" Tim asked.

"Honestly, Tim, our initial intelligence gathering is that this thing fizzled out pretty quickly," Jack said. "All of the leadership for the city is in custody, police chief is dead, bunch of rioters died in that bomb blast or were shot. I think they didn't count on us responding to them that directly, like we would just roll over and let this happen."

"We can't let down our guard completely, but you are probably right on that. You said the police chief is dead?"

"Yes, looks like she was shot, not sure by who yet," Jack said.

"Do we care?" Tim said, only half-jokingly.

"We will do our due diligence in investigating it," Jack responded. "If it was one of my guys, I am already looking at this as justified. She was leading an insurgency..."

"Don't even bother explaining, Jack, this is a non-issue if it was one of our people," Tim interrupted.

42.

"Good morning, Dante," Capo sounded delighted answering the phone, "what a wonderful new day it is, no?"

"Capo, they are asking about you by name," Dante half whispered, his anger visible in his voice, "this was not ever supposed to get traced back to us. Not even 24 hours into it and they are already asking me about you, by name!"

"Well, what did you tell them?" he asked, obviously less concerned about the revelation than Dante was, but still surprised his name had come up.

"I told them I would check into it, Capo," he said sarcastically. "There was not supposed to be anything coming back to the base, or to you, and certainly not to me. This was supposed to look like a terrorist attack, coordinating it with our friends in Austin making a mess of their capitol. It was supposed to break the back of the Nazis and bigots in the rural areas. What the hell happened?"

"We were planning exactly that, but we had some issues along the way and we just pushed along trying to do maximum damage," Capo said. "We hit them very hard, Dante, very hard. They will not soon forget."

"Not soon forget what? They were not supposed to *know* anything. The plan was to weaken them, make the people of Texas think their government could not protect them, make them vulnerable to a socialist takeover from within," Dante was no longer whispering, but almost yelling. "You really think that Texas will sit by and do nothing if they know we directly attacked them?"

"I think they will think twice after the damage we did to them, maybe if they know we did it that is not such a bad thing," Capo said.

"Are you insane?" Dante was growing more anxious by the minute. "Not such a bad thing? It will be an awful thing, the worst thing possible. Stay in your damn lane, Capo. You train them and equip them. You leave the political strategy to me, you leave the timing up to me, you leave the permission up to me!"

"Whatever you say boss." Capo said dismissively. "You want me to wait on sending the other buses then?"

"Jesus, Capo. There will be no more sending of buses, are we clear?"

"Sure, should we wait on Phase 2 then as well?" Capo asked.

"Capo, do nothing, absolutely nothing for right now. Do nothing at all until you hear otherwise from me," Dante said and then hung up the phone without waiting for an answer.

Capo looked at his phone, shrugged, and then extended his middle finger at it as though Dante were looking at him through it. "This is what I think of you and your pussyfoot ideas, Dante."

Capo got into his Cadillac and left the base, waving to the guard at the gate as he left. He lit a large Cuban cigar and drove toward his home with the windows down. Savoring the cigar made him appreciate the previous President and his affection for the communist government of Cuba. Capo was thankful for his reestablishing of relations with Cuba every time he looked the humidor full of cigars he now had at home, if for nothing else. This President had damaged those relations again, so he was glad he stocked up before the election.

Home would always be Mexico, where he grew up, but California was very nice and he had done well for himself. Someday, he thought, he would be in a position of even more power, and California would be at the forefront of power in what would remain of this country. It might even be its own country, or maybe a part of Mexico. Capo was satisfied with himself, almost as much as he was disgusted with Dante's weakness. The man had no business running a state like California. This plan was going to take courage, and Dante seemed in short supply of that.

The drive home was only a few minutes, and he parked his car in the driveway and walked up to the front door. He had no wife or children, having decided this kind of life would need his full attention. Maybe once this was over, once he was in power, he might decide to have a family. He wanted to have kids, but he could wait until he was able to raise them in a society he approved of. California was mostly becoming that society, but he needed to cement it by removing even the possibility of it ever reverting through federal involvement. Federal courts were still a problem. A progressive United States would be best, but he would settle for a separate People's Republic of California if that weren't possible.

To leftists like himself, this new President had been helpful to the cause, even if unwittingly. Capo, and all of those on the left, hated him deeply. They considered him a Nazi and a bigot, and anyone who voted for him or supported him was cast as one as well. However, his non-interventionist philosophy when it came to states' rights had allowed California to lurch toward socialism further than ever before, and the nullification position the state now operated under combined with almost no federal interference was quickly making the dream of a socialist state into a reality.

Tactics had to change in order to finish this mission. It was no longer as simple as making the right cower in fear of being seen as something vile. Political correctness had begun to wear out its usefulness some time ago, and was replaced instead with outright lies. Even that tactic was beginning to lose ground. Allegations of sexual misconduct were no longer effective against those on the right after famously failing to take down a Supreme Court justice nominee. Such allegations against conservatives were now even less effective than calling them racists, the words and accusations no longer held any meaning or importance. The return to a presumption of innocence as well as the flagrant misuse of the terms and fraudulent accusations levied from the Left rendered insults such as Nazi, bigot, and racist, largely impotent.

A ballot initiative next week would determine if the official name of the state would change from the Republic of California to the Socialist Republic of California. Polls showed an 87% likelihood of it passing. This President had been better for the Left in that regard than even they were willing to admit. Progress toward socialism would have been slow if anyone else from either party or political philosophy had been elected. It was the perfect storm right now, and Capo intended to make the most of it, to capitalize on the Left's fury and motivation, to turn emotion into action.

The only state that even seemed interested in pursuing a challenge to California's nullification position was Texas. Both senators from State of Texas had introduced a bill that would sanction California through interstate trade restrictions for the state's continued refusal to halt abortions. California's nullification position meant that the state had not stopped providing abortions, often at taxpayer expense, even after they were declared illegal by the Supreme Court. California was now attracting those seeking an abortion from all over the country. Capo was going to see to it that Texans changed their minds as well. When he was done, Texas would be brought to its knees, maybe even to the point of considering the California ways of doing things. Either way, California would be free to pursue a socialist empire free from interference.

As Capo walked into the house, he dialed a number from his cell phone.

"Hi there, Capo, how are you?" the voice on the other end greeted.

"Professor Stevens, my friend, life is good," Capo replied. "How is our little experiment going?"

"Almost done, Capo, when you can you come see me?" Don Stevens replied. Don Stevens was a biology professor at UCLA, and a longtime friend of Capo's having worked on several socialist candidate campaigns together. Capo and Don trusted one another completely, they were true believers in the movement.

"I was planning to come out tomorrow, is that good for you?"

"That will be just fine," Don said. "You are going to be very happy, Capo. Very happy indeed."

43.

Mac and his team arrived in the middle of the night on the suburban Los Angeles street where Capo lived. They took turns watching his house through Steiner binoculars, documenting anything of interest. The neighborhood was absolutely quiet, everything around the team was asleep. They took one-hour shifts and in the positions of surveillance or security while other two rested. One team took up a position near the expressway entrances while the other was watching Capo's house. If Capo were to move, the other team was to move in to follow so as not to alert Capo to the team nearest his house.

A roving surveillance was planned for the beginning of the day. The teams would gather as much intelligence as possible, but the plan was to kidnap Capo on his way home this evening, after he went to the Guard base or anywhere else. The rest of the intelligence would be gathered more personally at a preselected location already prepared for the interrogation.

At about 6am, Capo came out of the house and got into his Cadillac. Mac sent a text to the other team:

Just saw a frog jump into the pond.

Capo was wearing dress slacks and a sport coat, not his military uniform.

Someone pick up some bread on the way home, please.

This next text prompted the teams to switch to their encrypted radios o. Mac keyed up the mic and said "frog still swimming, standby for direction."

The Cadillac pulled out of the driveway and began moving. Mac waited until it turned right at the end of the street before pulling away from the curb to follow, the other team already moving to intercept the vehicle as it came out onto the main road. After following for some distance, the two switched and Mac picked up the tail again. For the next few minutes, Mac updated the other team by radio of their location, allowing them to move into place and to be ready to pick up the tail if Mac had to pull off. Distance and vehicles in between theirs and Capo's made it highly unlikely Capo would detect that he was being followed. The two teams following him were experts in this craft, and Capo was not.

After a trip through the drive-thru for breakfast, the big Cadillac finally pulled into the UCLA campus near the biology department. Mac stopped at the street light and let Seth out on foot. He then continued on the street ahead in order to keep from appearing like he was following Capo. Seth moved on foot toward the department, his hoodie preventing anyone from seeing that he was fixated on where the Cadillac was parking.

Once he parked in the faculty parking spot right in front of the building's entrance, Capo got out of the car and walked in, carrying a cup of coffee and not bothering to look around at all. Seth walked up toward the entrance, but waited until Capo was out of sight. He then went over to the Cadillac and peered inside. There was nothing out of the ordinary that he could see. He paid careful attention to the areas between the seats and on the floorboards, looking for a gun, but saw none.

Glancing around him, Seth looked for any security or campus police vehicles. Seeing none, he walked to the entrance of the biology department building and went in the same door he had seen Capo enter. It was still early, and there were not many people inside as classes had not yet begun. An occasional student would walk by, visibly tired without exception and usually wearing pajamas. Seth wondered for a moment if there was a dorm attached to the biology building, but resigned himself to the fact that this was just how college students dressed these days. He pulled down his hoodie as to not draw attention, and moved through the halls listening intently for people talking. Outside of room 1401A, he heard a hearty laugh and then a voice.

"Don, you are too good at this," Capo said.

Seth paused outside the door, checking the hallways for anyone who might notice him lurking around.

"Capo, this was really not that hard," Professor Stevens laughed. "We had all the materials, it was making it into a stable aerosol delivery system that was most challenging, but it is done."

Seth pulled a small notebook from his sweatshirt pocket along with a bullet pen. He noted the room number and what was said. An interior door closed and he could no longer hear the conversation that was going on. For a second, he contemplated sneaking further in but thought better of it. He moved toward the entrance from which he came and found a directory. Looking at office number 1401A, he saw it listed to "Professor Don Stevens, PhD, Head of Research." Writing this down, he walked out into the parking lot and called for Mac to pick him up.

He walked off the campus to a parking lot across the street and jumped in as Mac pulled up. "How'd it go?" Mac asked.

"He is meeting with a biology professor, I have the name and room number," Seth said. "They sounded like they were friends, but they were talking about an aerosol delivery system before they shut the door and I couldn't hear them anymore."

"Hmm," Mac said. "That does not sound good at all."

"No," Seth replied. "I think we need to have the other team grab that professor too."

"Agreed," Mac said.

"Same here," said Joe.

"Concur," came David's reply.

Mac got on the radio with the other teams and gave them the location and identity of an additional target for capture. They responded that they were on their way, and were advised to wait until after confirmation that Capo had left before doing anything. Mac pulled into the campus parking lot and selected an inconspicuous parking spot to watch the Cadillac, still parked in the faculty spot in front of the building. The team stayed alert for any campus security or police that might find an SUV full of middle-aged men sitting in a college campus parking lot suspicious.

A few minutes later, Capo came walking out of the building and put the key in his door without looking around, a sign that Mac knew marked him as an amateur. As the Cadillac backed out of the parking spot, Mac sent a text to the second team.

1401A. Take the package with you now.

He was closing in on the traffic light to pull out of the parking with two cars between his team and the Cadillac. The second team pulled into the parking lot just as the light turned green and they began to move forward, neither driver looked at the other as they passed. Mac watched in the side view mirror as the other team pulled into the same spot Capo had been parked in and saw three men disembark from the vehicle and head into the building, and then he focused his attention on the Cadillac.

"You think he's headed for the base?" Seth asked.

"I don't know, but we will take him on the first chance we get," Mac said. "If he goes to the base, that might mean taking him at his house later this evening, otherwise we will grab him first chance."

"Looks like we might be in luck," Seth said as the Cadillac pulled off the road and into the alleyway to the rear of a shopping mall. Mac stopped in the street and Seth jumped out of the car and jogged toward the rear of the strip mall to follow on foot. As he turned the corner, the Cadillac was parked in front of the dumpsters behind the first store, not visible from the street, and partially blocking the view of Capo as he urinated behind the dumpster.

Seth moved quickly, Capo's back was to him as he approached.

"Senor Rodriguez?" Seth said as he neared Capo.

Capo was just zipping up his pants as he heard his name called and turned with a start. "Yes?"

Seth's collapsible ASP baton opened while he swung forward, snapping to full extension just before contact as the tip smashed into Capo's jaw bone right at the juncture with his ear. Capo crashed to the ground, instantly unconscious.

Seth collapsed his baton and looked around quickly. Mac pulled down the alleyway from the other direction, having circled the strip mall, and Joe and David jumped out to help Seth. They tossed him into the back of the SUV, zip-tied his hands together, and put a burlap sack over his head. David stayed in the back with the new cargo and they pulled away in a matter of seconds. Just as they got onto the road, Mac received a text message from the other team. *Picked up a package, heading home.*

Clark came into the office and sat at the table with Grace and Ray, placing his cellphone in the center.

"Tim, I have Ray Tucker here from the Liberty Policy Foundation, he has been sworn to secrecy," Clark said into the phone's speaker.

"Ray, thank you for helping out with this," the governor's voice came over the speakerphone.

"It is an honor, sir," Ray said.

The governor quickly gave an update on what was known so far and the results of the investigations at the scenes of the explosions as well as the destroyed buses in Texas and New Mexico.

"The explosives and weapons recovered from the buses were all military-grade, and made in the United States for the US military," Tim said. "The firearms register back to the California National Guard. Some were destroyed completely, but others were perfectly functional and traceable. None of the explosives or weapons have been reported stolen. The buses themselves had no identifying marks or VIN tags and were apparently custom made similar to the road tour buses used by bands."

"Circumstantial evidence right now, Tim," Clark said.

"Right, we have nothing to tie them directly to Dante," Tim said.

Ray looked a bit surprised, "Dante Malone?"

"Yes, if we are going to respond in any way to California, we need to tie this directly to the Governor's office, not just some fringe group, even if they are some rogue unit of the California Guard," Tim responded.

"Yes, that would make sense, sir," Ray said. "If it is just a fringe group or even a few rogue soldiers, it would be California's responsibility to deal with it internally, not ours."

"But if it does go back to Malone, what are your thoughts, Ray?" Grace asked.

"Well," Ray began, "Texans would likely be supportive of a retaliatory response of some sort. It would be justified, and politically popular. It would also possibly be preventative and thereby further justified. Preventative in the sense that we would be attempting to preempt another attack."

"I think you are right, Ray," Tim said. "What is an alternative option in your view?"

Ray paused, then said, "Perhaps a retaliatory strike, but covert, and a denial of our involvement at all. Similar to Israeli policy."

"Hmm, interesting," Tim said. "What would be the benefit of doing it that way?"

"If it were an open secret that California was involved, then the open secret that we retaliated might not be too frowned upon by the general public outside of Texas, and might minimize the chances of an escalation by either side," Ray said. "An open response, one where we announce our involvement or take credit for a strike, might be seen as the start of a war, depending of course on a lot of variables."

"Ok, everyone, we have a lot to think about," Tim said, "we can do this again tomorrow morning. Maybe we will know more by then."

The phone disconnected. Clark looked at Ray and said "Thank you, this is helpful for all of us. There are some really important decisions being made right now, you are helping us make them."

"Truly honored, sir," Ray said. "Can I ask you, do we have any intelligence yet that the governor of California was involved in this in any way?"

"We are working on that," Grace said, smiling in a way that let Ray know she knew a little more than she was willing to tell him yet. He noticed that her eyes were green for the first time, and that there was a softness to them that was contrary to the assertiveness of her personality. "If we were to use a covert response, Ray, would it be feasible to use outside groups sympathetic to the operation rather than our own Texas National Guard or DPS Anti-terror Unit?"

"What kind of outside groups do you mean?" Ray asked.

"Militias," Grace said, her eye contact with him unbroken.

"Let me give that some thought, Grace. I hadn't considered that possibility, but my initial thoughts are that it makes a lot of sense," Ray said after a pause. "The militias are not bound by any constraints the government would be, they are probably equally skilled, and there are no disclosure requirements or freedom of information requests that would be binding on such an organization."

"Those were my thoughts too," said Clark. "Ray, we have been in contact with some militia elements for several years now, ever since the talks of a possible secession were popular. There had been little need to engage with them recently because the idea of secession was less appealing with the new administration in the White House. People who were ramped up for it under the old administration are mostly content under this one."

"Are the elements trustworthy?" Ray asked.

"Very," Grace replied. "The group we unofficially work with is highly trained, made up of almost all former military or law enforcement."

"What has their response been so far?" Ray asked.

"They are gathering intelligence right now," Clark said. "We are hoping that they will give us information soon to act on."

45.

Jack was leaning back in his chair, one cowboy boot up on Tim's desk, working his way through emails on his phone. Tim stood up from his desk and stretched.

"I am going to walk to the capitol for a minute, Jack."

"I'll go with you," Jack said, jumping to his feet.

The pair walked into an underground tunnel that went to the capitol directly from the governor's office. They walked quickly, grateful to be out of the other office for a change a scenery. This stretch of tunnel was secured, it was for the Governor and his personnel to move to and from the capitol building quickly and had no access for the public. When they approached the tunnel door leading out into Governor's private office inside the capitol, Tim entered the passcode and the door swung inward. They were startled briefly to see two men in the office, dressed all in black. The intruders both reached for baseball bats that were resting against the desk. Tim brushed his suit jacket aside and smoothly drew his 1911. It barked a split second before Jack's Glock did, and both intruders fell dead to floor.

Tim and Jack cleared the remainder of the office and the closet, looking for other unwanted guests. The glass on the entrance door had been broken, and there was garbage all over the office. The two looked to have been living there since the other night's events, based on the condition of the office. Tim did not keep any sensitive documents in the capitol office, so the papers strewn about the floor were of little concern to him. They checked both bodies for identification, but found none.

"I will call it in," Jack said, "but we should head back, Tim. This area is obviously not secure."

Jack spoke to a dispatcher on their way back through the tunnel. Tim was quiet. He had been involved in a couple of shootings as a police officer, but assumed that part of his life was over after entering politics. He was realizing that this might be a new sort of normal for Texans, himself included. He reminded himself that they were not at war, but couldn't help adding to that thought a reminder that war could be just around the corner.

"I have some investigators heading over there, Tim," Jack said after hanging up the phone. "They will come by later to get our statement."

"Yes, no problem," Tim said. He looked at Jack with a slight smirk on his face and said "why were you so slow on the draw back there?"

Jack laughed out loud and just shook his head. "Those two must have holed up there since the riot, I suppose none of our security personnel thought to check your office since you were over in the mansion."

"Could have just been vandals, too," Tim said. "This is going to be a different place for a while, Jack."

"Yes, I suppose it is," Jack nodded. "Do you have any sensitive documents over there, should I have the team secure them?"

"No, nothing," Tim said. "That office is mostly a break area for my staff, all our work and papers are here in the mansion. We don't even have a computer in there unless we bring one with us."

"Ok, good," Jack said as they got back to the office. "Probably keep it that way for now. I will have my people go through the whole building again to make sure we have cleared it out. How long before you want to go back to opening it around the clock like it used to be?"

"Not sure, Jack," Tim said looking over at him. "Not sure if we be doing that anytime soon, unfortunately." Tim hated saying it, keeping the capitol open all the time was important, it was the people's house and it should be welcoming, day or night. Tim quietly wished he could be sure it would one day return to that, but he was not so sure it ever would.

46.

Capo was afraid of the water. He could not swim and the fear of drowning was a phobia that plagued him since he was a child. He watched as the men with balaclavas covering their faces brought in several five-gallon water bottles and a towel, and he knew what was coming. For a fleeting moment he thought about the fact that these men could not possibly know of his fear of water, that he might be able to pretend the sight of the water did not bother him. He quickly dismissed that bravado as the terror washed over him like a wave.

"You, you, you, don't need to do this my friends," he stuttered. "What information are you wanting?"

The men did not answer him, they moved about like shadows. He looked around but could barely see beyond the bright light aimed in face. The floors were concrete and the echo off the walls made him believe they were metal. He was confident that he was in a storage locker of some sort, but he had no idea where. He could see two men standing before him now. One was wetting the towel. Capo's heart began to race.

"My friends, really, there is no need," he began to plead.

"Capo," said one of the men, though he was not sure which because their faces were covered. "Capo, we want you to know that we are serious. In order to show that, we are going to cause you significant pain and terror before we even ask you one question."

"There is no need for me to doubt your seriousness, my friends," Capo pleaded. "What is it you want to know?"

"Perhaps you could avoid this, if you were to tell us what *you* think we want to know," the shadowy figure said. "That would demonstrate to us that we don't have to do this because it would show your willingness to cooperate."

"You might want to know the troop strength at my base, or maybe my bank account information," Capo offered nervously.

"See, Capo, for a moment I thought you would not play games with us," the masked man said almost laughing.

The men reclined Capo's chair so that he was almost lying flat, then used a leather belt to strap his head down to the back of the reclined platform. Capo protested with near screams. One of the men held the towel over Capo's face while the other began pouring water over it. Capo screamed, interrupted by gurgling, and then screamed again. He was drowning, he was sure of it. Terror and panic racked his body as he convulsed and choked on the water. The men stopped pouring the water and removed the towel from Capo's face. They returned his chair to an upright position. Capo gagged and cried.

"Capo, we are going to ask you a few questions now," one of the men whispered into his ear. "If you so much as hesitate to answer them, we will drown you, do you understand?"

"Si, yes, yes," Capo said in between gasps for air. "Whatever you want to know, just do not do that again, please."

The interrogator brought over a dry towel and dabbed Capo's face to dry it. He knelt down in front of Capo, his ice blue eyes the only part of his face Capo could see behind the balaclava.

"Capo, how are you involved in the bombings, the buses, and the attacks in Texas?" The man asked.

"I only let those maniacs use the base, that is all," Capo said. His eyes grew wide as the other man slid the water jug closer. "I am telling you the truth!"

"Who told you to let them use the base, and who are the maniacs you are referring to?"

"Bunch of leftists and communists, they call themselves The Resistance or some crap like that," Capo said, desperate to distance himself from the operation.

"And Professor Stevens, we have him in another room, is he going to tell us the same thing?" the interrogator asked.

"He better!" Capo's surprise at the mention of the professor's name quickly became anxiety and he grew more animated. "He had some chemicals or something he wanted me to give to the group, that's all."

"I thought you only allowed them some space?" the interrogator said. The water moved closer.

"I did, I did, I swear I did," Capo pleaded. "He was working on some weapon for The Resistance. He can tell you all about it, I know very little about it."

"He already has, so choose your words carefully. How is Dante Malone connected to you?" the interrogator asked.

Capo hesitated, looked at the water jug, and then at the floor. He was ashamed of his fear, but not enough to go through another round of waterboarding.

"He told me to let The Resistance use the base, he is more connected to them than I am," Capo said slowly. It was a partial lie, but one that these men would not punish him for even if they knew.

"Dante Malone, the governor of California, ordered you to give aid and shelter to terrorists planning to attack the state of Texas?" the interrogator asked in more of a statement than a question.

Capo looked up at him, paused for a moment, then nodded his head and said, "Yes."

47.

Grace, Clark, and Ray sat in front of the computer monitor watching the recording of Capo's interrogation through an encrypted connection. Before they could begin discussing it, a second video was sent of the professor's confession. The professor answered every question immediately without hesitation, the militia's interrogators had not even had to threaten him because he gave in so easily. Capo had at least offered some resistance, even if it was very little. When the second video ended, all three leaned back in their chairs.

"The governor of California orchestrated this," Ray said in disbelief.

"Sure looks that way," Clark nodded.

"Ray, what are your thoughts on the Israeli policy model you floated yesterday?" asked Grace. "The one where we hit them but never acknowledge it publicly."

"Well, the way I see it would be that there are three options," Ray began. "The first option would be to have a non-government entity, the militias for example, conduct the retaliation and we deny any involvement at all. The problem there is that the militia doing the strike would be subject to federal terrorism laws." Grace and Clark were looking at him intently, but it was Grace's stare that threatened to derail his thoughts. "They could be in real trouble."

"The second option is to hit them with the Texas National Guard in a limited fashion," he continued. "I am not a military strategist, so you will need others to fill in those details, but we would have much more control over what the response looked like in this scenario. The problem here is deniability, we would just have to refuse to comment because denying it would not be popular with any side if they knew we were lying. The Israelis do this consistently, no confirmation or denial. They just move on with their business after the strike."

"The third option is a joint effort between the Guard and the militias," Ray said. "Perhaps a high profile strike on the California Guard base or some other priority target and," Ray paused, looking at the two before continuing. "And, perhaps the Governor." Neither Clark nor Grace flinched. "The militias could take out the biology department at UCLA, and hit a few strategic targets such as some of their openly antagonistic lawmakers maybe."

"You are thinking this out as we go along, Ray?" Grace laughed. "It sounds like you have thought this through before."

"I am just thinking out loud right now," he smiled. "Assassinating a sitting governor is a major response, and I need to think through the ramifications on that. We rarely consider that option even in terms of foreign leaders."

"Ray, could you write out a rough outline for all three scenarios?" Clark asked. "I want to get this to the governor as soon as possible for his consideration."

"Yes, I will get on it right away," Ray said. "Is there a particular one you want me to focus on more than the others?"

Grace and Clark looked at each other before Grace answered, "the third one. Detail the third one more than the other two."

48.

Dante's chief of staff ran into the governor's office and turned on the big screen television. CNN has a full screen video it was playing.

"State your name and rank," a digitally altered voice said off camera. Capo's face and a copy of today's LA Times took up the whole screen. He looked scared, but managed to control his voice with his answer.

"My name is Emmanuelle Rodrigues, or Capo, and I am the base commander for the California National Guard in Los Angeles," he said, occasionally glancing at the floor.

"What is The Resistance?" the off screen voice asked.

"A group of progressives trying to take over this country through violence," Capo said, his voice trailing off on the last word.

"And your relationship to them?"

"I allowed them to stay, train, and access weapons at my base," Capo looked directly at the camera now.

"Did you do this on your own?" the digital voice asked in its monotone and robotic staccato.

"No, I was ordered to," Capo's eyes did not waiver.

"By whom?"

"Dante Malone, the governor of California, my Commander in Chief," Capo said without looking away.

Dante gasped, he felt his mouth go dry. All eyes in the room turned to him.

"What were the orders you dutifully followed, Commander Rodriguez?"

"Prepare, support, train, and equip The Resistance for an attack on Texas," he replied without hesitation."

The screen went black and commentator came into view wide-eyed and too stunned to talk.

"Turn it off!" Dante told his chief of staff. "Leave my office, please."

Dante's hands were shaking violently as he dialed the number himself to call Tim Leland. When his secretary told him he was unavailable, Dante left a pleading message about Capo being a rogue and telling terrible lies and how he would deal with him himself. When he set the phone in its cradle, he put his elbows on the desk and his face in his hands. Immediately, his mind went to work on how to spin this. Whatever plan he chose would have to be in line with what he just left on the message, but he could not be sure there would be no more videos that contradict what he said.

It should be easy to deny, no one would believe a sitting governor was responsible for a violent attack on another state. The only problem Dante could think of right now was the fact that the group identified as The Resistance was a prominent supporter of his, and rather than renouncing their support he had embraced it. He was going to catch some of the blame on this no matter what happened. Certainly it would be better to appear associated with the group and let them take the blame for the attack than to be blamed for coordinating the attack himself.

Dante picked up his phone again, paused and then put it back down. That Leland was a hot-headed Texan for sure, Dante thought. He wasn't sure what this would bring. The economic war between the two states had been hurting California far more than it did Texas, even more than Dante had publicly admitted. Dante was sure that Leland's response would be economic sanctions, even if no one could tie the attacks to him with evidence outside of Capo's video.

Dante seethed at the thought of Capo. He hoped whoever had him right now would kill him. He wondered how a commander of a military base could have been so sloppy, so indiscreet with the operations entrusted to him. Capo's capture and cowardly confession made any future operations much more difficult. Dante knew this was the end of covert attacks and that he could not even attempt another attack in the near future due to the heat this one is surely going to bring, and that delay will negate the terror and damage done by this attack. Texans will have rebuilt their damaged areas and strengthened their resolve by then and any new initiative by The Resistance would be like starting from square one. He tapped the desk with his finger, then picked up the phone again.

49.

The trio gathered around a television in the makeshift office at the DPS headquarters in Waco. Ray leaned back at the end of it with an astonished look on his face. Grace glanced over at Clark, and then focused on Ray.

"Let us know what you think, Ray," she said.

"Well," Ray began after a long pause, "this is unprecedented for sure. If we have no reason to doubt he is telling the truth, then Governor Leland doesn't need to make much more of a case on this, the nation already is primed to believe it was Malone. We can announce whatever sanctions he thinks are appropriate as our official response."

"And?" Grace asked, knowing there was more than that.

"And unofficially we hit them back, hard," Ray suggested.

"What would that look like?" Clark asked, leaning toward him.

"My suggestion is that we enlist the militias, there are a lot of them here in Texas, to do some covert operations on the ground over there, then deny any involvement outright, or at least refuse to comment on it. Any official action we take should not be denied, but we will refuse to confirm it, or even discuss it," Ray said.

"We have a militia group that is willing to work with us, Ray," Grace said after nodding to Clark. "In fact, they are already working with us."

Ray looked a little surprised, but not overly so. "Ok, good, that cuts out one of the steps that I was going to suggest. If they are already vetted, then swift action is probably best."

"What are your thoughts on targets?" Clark asked.

"That's probably best left to your military folks, it's outside my wheelhouse," Ray admitted.

"But the optics of the attacks are not outside your wheelhouse, what would be too much, or too far?" Grace asked.

"Quite frankly, I don't know that there is a 'too much' or 'too far' at this point," Ray said. "They attacked our state, blew up parts of our cities, killed our police officers and innocent civilians. There is no response that is 'too far'."

"Assassinations?" Clark asked. "You mentioned that as a possible option last time."

"So long as we can plausibly deny involvement, perfectly acceptable," Ray said. "This is warfare, righteous warfare in the defense of our citizens. What they did was murder, and Malone was an accomplice to that murder. We could make the argument that it is war. If anyone is to be condemned at the end of this, no matter how it plays out, it is them. California is unlikely to respond at all, they will not want to draw any more attention to this than they already have."

"What would you do with the guy in that video if we had him?" Grace asked.

"Do we have him?" Ray was genuinely surprised at this revelation.

"If we did," Grace said, "what would we do with him?"

"Well, for now, we would hold him in custody and extract more intelligence from him," Ray said. "Eventually, we would probably have to do a military tribunal, I guess. I am not sure on that part, but I would definitely keep him for intel."

When the video of UCLA professor Don Stevens came on the screen a moment later, the trio looked to the television again. The professor's confession required no questions from a digitally altered voice as he gave one long monologue about building an aerosol dispersion unit for anthrax intended to hit five major Texas cities at the directions of Dante Malone, the governor of California. At the end of it, he looked at the camera and said, "I'm sorry."

50.

The President was at his desk in the Oval Office for a live press conference. He looked concerned, but he was confident. Pressure did not affect him like it did most people, and he felt little need to intervene in this situation even now. He was an absolutist when it came to the sovereignty of the states, and he felt Texas and California should figure this out between themselves. His staff, however, encouraged him to at least offer to host a summit between the two states at the White House, with an offer to mediate.

"I ask that all sides remain calm until we know exactly what has happened in the great state of Texas," he began. "California and Texas, two of our largest and greatest states, must come together to solve the differences between them peacefully and permanently. I offer to both governors Leland and Malone all the time and space they need here at the White House to discuss this situation, and will be happy to mediate the talks if they so choose. I look forward to hearing from both of them."

He took no questions from the press and left the room immediately.

Immediately after the broadcast, Governor Malone appeared at his own press conference. He was visibly nervous as he spoke.

"I gratefully accept the President's offer to come to the White House to discuss the horrible events that occurred in Texas a few days ago. But I request that he also invite other governors to attend, being that California as a state had nothing to do with the attack and has no need to have a meeting mediated with the governor of Texas. We should all come together to help out Texas in its time of need, not just California. The time and date of this summit can be whatever is convenient for Governor Leland, I will make myself available even on a moment's notice. I will not be taking any questions." Dante rushed off the platform and out of the room amidst screaming questions from reporters.

For the next fifteen minutes news commentators on all stations rabidly speculated on all of the revelations of the previous several hours. Two commentators on a network known for its radical progressive bias even called for the impeachment of the President over the attack, claiming it was somehow a federal government conspiracy to drive a wedge between the two states and paint California in a bad light.

Governor Leland addressed the camera from behind the desk in his office. He looked stern, but not nervous. Behind him, only the Texas flag was visible.

"Thank you for the invitation, Mr. President, but Texas has no need for a mediator and is uninterested in discussing anything of any sort with the governor of California. The people of Texas have already begun their recovery, and have voiced their expectation that California pay a price for its part in these deadly attacks. I am announcing the following sanctions against California effective immediately," Tim said with a look on his face that left no one watching unsure of the seriousness of his resolve. "First, there will be no oil sales to California from Texas. Second, California driver's licenses and concealed carry licenses will no longer be recognized in the state of Texas. Commercial truck drivers, tourists, or anyone else holding a California driver's license will no longer be allowed to operate a vehicle in Texas. Those caught driving will be arrested for operating a vehicle without a license. Third, all products produced by California, or imported by California and shipped elsewhere will not be allowed into the state of Texas, no internet sales from a business in California can be shipped here either. We may have more sanctions coming, but this is a pretty good start." Tim paused for a moment then continued. "The full connection of the State of California to the attacks on Texas are still being investigated, but the evidence thus far is clear in its implication of the Governor of California."

Tim took no questions, in part because there was no press in his office other than the single camera crew used for the conference. The mansion and the capitol were still on lockdown.

51.

The Speaker of the State Assembly lived just outside Sacramento in a beautiful southwestern style mansion. The orange clay roof tiles and white stucco walls of the stately manor were surrounded by six foot stone walls and an electric security gate that prevented access to the winding driveway leading to the four-car garage. In the garage were an assortment of fine German automobiles. The view from the second floor balcony looked across the road at the rolling hills, covered in patches of trees.

Maxwell Dunham rose from the steam of his whirlpool tub and dried himself off. He contemplated what the day's events meant. Dante, he concluded, was an idiot. Max was grateful that he had never entertained a meeting or even a conversation with Capo, who proved most disappointing. This whole thing was likely to take down Dante, but probably not the movement they had started together, certainly The Resistance would survive as an ideology. That wasn't exactly true, he conceded to himself, the movement was not really their doing, but its rise to prominence certainly was. This was just the beginning. Maxwell calculated that Dante would be out and he would ascend to the governor's seat by some means, elected or otherwise, and then the real campaign against those Nazi's and bigots in Texas would begin. Once they hammered Texas into submission, the other states would fall in line and California would be the new Washington DC. Dante's departure could not come soon enough. Maxwell was sure that Dante did not have the courage to see this through, and that he was likely in a full panic already.

Maxwell put on a heavy white robe and moved out to the balcony with a cigar in one hand and a glass of scotch in the other. He had been Speaker for eight years, the power making him even more arrogant than before, which was quite the feat. He took a puff on the cigar, alternately sipping his scotch. His friends would have scoffed at the routine, telling him he was ruining the fine smoothness of his very expensive scotch with the smoke from the Cuban cigar, that the two experiences should be enjoyed separately. Max liked the extra burn from the scotch that the smoke provided.

He leaned against the railing of the balcony briefly, admiring the view of the hills and congratulating himself on the life he had achieved. Inside, his girlfriend was waiting in the bedroom. Twenty years his junior, she was ready to meet any demands he might have. Certainly, life was very good. Dante's foolishness, ironically might prove very beneficial to him personally. Dante was useful only as the public face of the movement, allowing Max to stay in the shadows of the grittiest parts of that game. Moving into the governor's seat would change that, but in a very good way. Max was a better politician than Dante, he would give a better message and be far more careful going forward with how much he allowed to be connected to the governor's office. Dante was indeed a damn fool.

In a patch of trees on the side of the hill directly across from the balcony lay Mac and Seth. Their ghillie suits made them all but invisible as they lay motionless, blending perfectly with the patch of grass they were in and breaking up the outline of their bodies and their rifles. A patch of nylon stocking stretched over the front lens of Seth's rifle scope and Mac's spotting scope, preventing the setting sun from providing any glint that could be detected by an observer. Nearly three football fields away, Maxwell would not have noticed them even if he looked directly at them. Seth turned the dial on his Nightforce scope to illuminate the reticule as dusk closed in and made it difficult to see the crosshairs against the background. Mac peered through his spotting scope.

The red dot settled just below Maxwell's nose in Seth's scope, some 280 yards away. He took a breath in and then exhaled slowly, pausing about half-way through the exhale and pressed the trigger. The .300 Win Mag thundered and Maxwell's head snapped back. The round continued through the glass doors behind him and lodged in the wall of the bathroom. Maxwell's body fell lifeless to floor the balcony, blood spilling through the wood slats in thick droplets onto the walkway below. The only sound left after the echo of the shot disappeared was the rain of blood onto the concrete.

"Hit," said Mac from behind his spotting scope.

Seth did not cycle the action on the Remington, deciding against ejecting the spent cartridge casing and providing anyone with evidence. He and Mac quietly exfiltrated from their hide, moving back against the hill and slowly around toward the far side where they could get to the awaiting vehicle. They did not speak on their way to the car, moving methodically and smoothly. Joe and David were waiting in the rental when they got there. Mac and Seth tore off their ghillie suits and stuffed them in the cargo area. They jumped into the back seat next to a handcuffed Capo, who was sleeping with his head against the window.

"Back to Texas?" David asked from the driver's seat.

"Yes, sir," Mac said. "Head for Amarillo, David. Capo needs to talk to someone there"

The team drove through the night, changing driver's as the others slept and only stopping for gas. Departing from Los Angeles, the second team made a quick drop off and also headed east for Texas.

At 7:00 a.m. the next morning, Professor Don Stevens was found handcuffed to the railing on the stairs of the FBI's Los Angeles field office. He was wearing a shirt that had "TERRORIST" written in large red letters on the front and back. He looked at the young Hispanic man and woman that made up the office's cleaning crew when they discovered him upon their arrival at the building pleadingly, and terrified. They looked back, also terrified. They spoke very little English, but they understood the word on his shirt very clearly.

52.

Dante was in a near panic as he hung up the phone. The news of Maxwell's assassination terrified him. Dante understood the dangers of being a public figure, and had plenty of security measures in place, but Maxwell had been so low profile in this operation. No one really knew how involved he had been, Dante had kept him out of meetings and calls with Capo and the leadership of The Resistance for the most part. He was a silent partner, but enormously effective.

Dante considered that Maxwell would be a natural target for someone who knew the depth of his involvement, but no one did. That was what terrified him, someone knew a lot more than they should, more than Dante considered possible. Maxwell had been an easy target for sure, especially for a sniper as it appeared to have been done. The fancy house by the hills, hanging out on the balcony, arrogance and foolishness. But *selecting* him as a target was the issue. If this was related, and it must be related, then Dante realized that his own life was in grave danger. He called a meeting with his security team for an hour from now. It was time for him to go into hiding.

Dante tried to calm himself down. There was the possibility that Maxwell's killing was not related to the events of the past week at all. Maxwell was involved with plenty of shady characters and questionable business endeavors that had nothing to do with The Resistance. Certainly it was possible that he had crossed one of those partners and this was the logical result. Dante concluded that he could not risk it. He would proceed as though his own life were in danger.

53.

Grace was looking at the television intently as the news discussed the assassination of the California Speaker of the State Assembly. Ray looked between the news and her, noticing here reaction was one of interest but not of surprise. He chose not to ask the question he already knew the answer to, instead letting his ears listen to the information while his eyes examined her beauty. Grace took a few notes on a yellow legal pad on the table in front of her. She looked up and Ray glanced away, slightly embarrassed for his staring. She smiled warmly at him, and the embarrassment faded.

"Ray, there are some things that I know you will know without having to ask," she said. "For those things, it is always better that they remain unsaid, don't you think?"

"Yes, definitely," Ray responded. He was now sure that his suspicion was true, that the assassination was connected to Texas in some way, but unofficially. He found that the prospect did not affect him at all, if anything he was somewhat proud that Texas had hit back. He did not stop to consider the morality of it, he made the decision when he had picked up Marie and the kids from the scene of the attack in Stephenville that this was war. It was a righteous and justified war. Killing in war was justified.

Ray was good at compartmentalizing things in his mind, a skill he used as a police officer throughout his career. There were things he left in those compartments from long ago, never opening them again. Surely there was some seepage from the compartments, tugging at the edge of his conscience demanding a hearing in his mind, but he resisted and thus kept his sanity for the most part. He figured that one day, all of those compartments would be examined in His presence, and there would be an accounting and a reckoning. He accepted that. Most police officers did.

Clark smiled at the two having an unspoken discussion in front of him. "Ray, would you say that this would have been a good official or unofficial move in regard to our discussion of the last few days?"

"Unofficial, for sure," Ray responded. "Everyone will assume this is related, but the connection will never be made officially and therefore there needs to be no comment on our part. If the sniper is as good as I assume he would be, there will be nothing of value to be found."

"Should the Governor comment at all?" Grace asked.

"I don't think so," Ray said, "I wouldn't even have him give condolences or a condemnation of the hit. Let everyone think it *might* have been us but give them nothing to say it *was* us."

Grace picked up a secure line and spoke to the Governor briefly, he concurred with Ray's recommendation.

"The Governor will make no comment at all on the assassination of the Speaker of the State Assembly in California," Grace told Ray and Clark after hanging up the phone. "He was initially inclined to a statement along the lines of 'you reap what you sow' but he has relented based on your recommendation," she laughed.

"He is a good leader," Ray chuckled. "The right person for the job at the right time, that doesn't always happen. We are lucky to have him."

Clark and Grace nodded. Ray was convinced that if this war were to spread that Tim Leland was a warrior that Texas could follow and trust. He recognized his own opinion was biased because the Governor was a former police officer, but Leland's character over the past week had justified that bias.

"I am starving, anyone want to go grab breakfast?" Grace asked.

"I am going to work on a couple things here, but could you grab me a breakfast taco while you are out?" Clark asked.

"I'm in," said Ray. "I can drive if you want."

Grace got into the passenger side of the Highlander and Ray pulled out of the lot and headed for downtown Waco. "Cracker Barrel sound good?"

"Sounds awesome," Grace said. "Thank you for your help on this, Ray. You have really been useful in informing our policy decisions."

"I'll be honest, Grace," Ray said, "I feel most of the time like you and Clark have already come to the policy decision before I even say a word. Not that this is a bad thing, I think every decision so far has been in line with what I would have recommended, but I feel like I am behind the curve."

"You are right, on some of the things we have been using your advice after the fact to critique our decisions, but not all of them," she told him. "Some of the really important ones have been based on your policy input."

"I am not complaining," Ray quickly qualified, "I am happy to be a part of this in any way you see fit. It was just an observation."

"An accurate one, which is why we enlisted you in the first place," Grace said. Her green eyes were soft as Ray glanced over at her.

At a table for two, Ray and Grace talked over breakfast and coffee. Ray marveled at how much Grace could eat and still maintain the slim athletic figure she had. He concluded she must work out incessantly, but where she would find the time escaped him.

"How many kids do you have, Ray?" she asked while looking down at her pancakes.

Ray was a little uncomfortable with the question. He had been divorced twice, a fact he was not proud of. While he was happier now that he was separated from Marie, he also knew deep down that many of the problems in their relationship were his fault. Most of those, however, were locked into one of those compartments. Questions like this threatened to pry open the door.

"A lot," he smiled. "I was married, twice, neither time turned out good."

She laughed without looking up. "How many is a lot?"

"Four with my second wife, and one with my first," he answered. The answer making him a little uncomfortable, the strained relationship with his children threatening to peek out from the door of a locked compartment. It had been years since he spoke to his oldest son from his first marriage, more than he cared to count right now. "Were you ever married?" he changed the subject by a degree.

"Almost, once," she said finally looking up at him. "It didn't work out."

Ray marveled at the difference in Grace while they were eating and talking. She seemed so much more relaxed, almost vulnerable. In the office she was a warrior, almost cold at times. Her warmth and softness in this setting was a stark contrast and Ray was even more attracted to her than ever. He pushed that into a compartment. Ray had made the decision after his divorce with Marie that there would be no more relationships. They never turned out good for anyone, not the woman and certainly not for himself. Still, he asked the obvious question, "why not?"

"The usual," she said. "I was caught up with law school and then looking for my career to begin, he wanted someone to stay home and raise kids and cook meals. I don't think there is anything wrong with a woman doing that at all, just not this woman," she laughed. Like the skilled lawyer she was, she shifted the questioning back on Ray. "Do you ever miss being a cop?"

"Every day," he said, taking a sip of his coffee. "Every day."

"Really?" she asked. "You seem so good at what you do now."

"Thank you," he smiled. "I like what I do, but I miss being on the street. Being a cop is the best job in the world if you do it right. What we are doing right now is a lot more like being a cop than a policy analyst if you want to know the truth."

"How so," Grace tilted her head inquisitively, irresistibly.

"We are protecting our people here, Grace," he said confidently. "We are serving and protecting at the highest level. I miss the street level work, but this is police work at its highest level, I really believe that."

"I had never thought of it that way," she said.

"You should, you are the highest law enforcement official in the state," he smiled at her.

She winked at him and smiled, and he nearly fell out of his chair.

54

Jack looked at Tim across the desk. Tim's reaction, or lack of it, told him everything he needed to know about the assassination that was being covered on the television screen in front of them.

"Grace says no comment on it," Tim said looking over at Jack.

"I agree," Jack replied. "Tim, there are parts of this response that I don't need to know about, I get that. But, I am on board with whatever direction you decide to take this, so don't feel the need to exclude me for my protection or yours."

Tim leaned back in his chair and looked at his friend, then breathed out a long sigh of relief. "Are you sure?" Tim asked slowly. "There is no turning back once you are inside, Jack."

"Positive," Jack replied without looking away.

"Ok, then, I am going to read you in on everything," Tim said leaning forward and folding his hands on the desk in front of him. "The videos were made and uploaded by the Hill Country Militia. Clark was a member, still is I suppose, and has strong connections with them. They are mostly former military and law enforcement, very well trained and very secretive. They are good at what they do."

Jack sat back in his seat, "Clark Bentley was in a militia?"

"Still is, I think," Tim replied. "He is kind of a badass, wouldn't know it from looking at him though."

"No kidding," Jack smiled.

"The group grabbed both the professor and that Capo guy the other day and got the video confessions that implicated Dante Malone in the attacks. They also implicated the Speaker, but they edited that out of the video, enough said about why and all that," Tim continued. "The plan is to use the sanctions in an official response, but also to partner with the militia in order to respond covertly with official deniability. We are watching the effectiveness of that now."

"Why covertly?" Jack asked. "My counter-terror teams would be happy to do this for you, just give the order."

"We are consulting with Ray Tucker from the Liberty Policy Foundation on our messaging and response. Do you know him?" Tim asked.

"Met him once," Jack said, "good guy, former cop, right?"

"Yes," Tim replied, "part of why I like him. But his recommendation was to hit back hard but leave no official footprint, take no responsibility even if it is shown to come back to us. He cautioned not to lie, not to deny it, but just refuse to acknowledge it officially. He said this is similar to the way the Israelis respond and thought it would be appropriate here."

"I see, I can't say I disagree," Jack nodded with a grin. "I am glad we are punching back hard, Tim. I think everyone would be glad if they knew the whole story."

"That is what Ray said, let them think we hit them back but never acknowledge it officially," Tim nodded.

"Y'all trust Ray on this, I assume he is the only one outside the top officials that know the inside out on it?" Jack asked.

"Completely," Tim said without hesitation. "Besides being a retired cop, he is part of Liberty Policy Foundation and they have never betrayed our confidence in any policy discussion, ever. They are a good group."

"Good point," Jack nodded.

"We are working on another response," Tim continued. "This one will test the whole concept pretty severely."

"How so?" Jack leaned forward.

"It will test our ability to not comment on something that is overtly obvious," Tim said. "This one would leave little doubt of our involvement, but without our claiming responsibility."

"Bigger than hitting the Speaker?" Jack asked.

"Who said we did that?" Tim smiled.

55.

Mac pulled the rental vehicle into the sally port of the Amarillo police station and met with James Thompson, who was standing in the port waiting.

"Good morning sir," Mac said extending his hand.

James took his hand and pulled him close, "good to see you, Mac!"

"Crazy times," Mac smiled at his old friend.

"Sure are, is that Capo in the back?"

"It is," Mac replied. "He is so soft already that he will tell you anything you want to know at this point."

"Good," James nodded. "I think I want to do a video of him and this piece of crap we have in custody here. Let them talk as much as they want."

"Is your guy talking anymore?" Mac asked.

"Mostly sleeps right now, APD shot him before capturing him, so he's pretty doped up most of the time" James said.

Capo was led to the cell where Adam Dansforth was sleeping, the noise of the door sliding open jarred him awake.

"Commander?" Adam asked, rubbing the sleep form his eyes. He was visibly encouraged, assuming Capo was here to rescue him.

Capo looked at him, gave him a nod, and then sat on the bunk across from him.

"I presume you two know each other," James said, "I will give you a little time to catch up and then we will all talk. How does that sound?"

Neither answered his question, waiting for him to leave the hallway before speaking. Once the door down the hall closed, they looked at each other.

"We are screwed, amigo," Capo said.

"I was hoping you were here to bring me home," Adam said, deflated.

"Ain't no one going home any time soon," Capo said. "We need to cooperate if we are going to have any chance of surviving, these Texans are pissed off. What happened to you anyway?"

"I got shot by an Amarillo cop during the attack on the mall, never even got a shot off," Adam said in a self-pitying voice. "You?"

"They kidnapped me off the street," Capo said. "They are very good, and they are very serious."

"In California, they captured you in California?" Adam asked, completely surprised by the statement.

"Yes, they made it there awfully quick, don't know how they put it together so fast," Capo looked suspiciously at Adam. "Unless of course, they had help."

"I'm sorry, Capo," Adam said tearfully, "I told them what I knew but they already had your name, I swear."

Capo looked around the jail cell, he assumed they could hear their conversation but had lost any interest in keeping secrets at this point. He was completely focused on survival now, the movement no longer meant anything to him.

"Whatever they want to know, you just tell them," Capo said in an almost fatherly tone. "No more resisting, don't lie to them. I am not so sure that they won't just kill us if we give them a reason."

"They told me they would," Adam said. "They said if there was another attack that I failed to tell them about, they would kill me."

"Well, there ain't no other attack coming any time soon," Capo said. "Dante is scared shitless right now. Wouldn't be surprised if he is in hiding already."

Adam was feeling a little lightheaded and went to lie down on his bunk again. Capo leaned back on his bunk, resting his head against the wall and closed his eyes to think. All he could think of right now was being a little boy in Mexico, sitting at the dinner table with his mamma and poppa waiting for his abuela to bring over the tamales and cornbread. It seemed a hundred years ago now, and every bad decision in his life had led him to this cell. If he could go back and start over, he would never have come to this country at all.

From the dispatch center, Mac, James, and Seth watched the closed circuit television and listened to the conversation in the cell.

"Best intel we can probably get from them at this point is finding out where Malone's hideout would be if he goes underground," Mac said, turning to James. "I don't have that information right now, do you?"

"No," James answered. "I had not actually considered that he would have a place like that, but maybe we can find out."

"Do you think he'd have an actual bunker?" Seth asked.

"He might," James replied, "depends on how long he has been planning this I would think. Let's let them rest a little, we will bring them in together in a little while and question them." Mac and Seth nodded in agreement.

Sergeant Rutherford walked into the room quietly and sat down. James introduced him to Mac and Seth.

"We are sorry for your loss, Sarge" Seth said, extending his hand.

"Thank you," Rutherford said, "it still hasn't sunk in yet. Fourteen officers, all gone. Men and women who won't go home to their families tonight. Faces I won't ever see at another roll call." His voice was soft now, his eyes red and watery.

Mac rose to go to the restroom, and paused to put his hand on Rutherford's shoulder. "They're in a better place now, brother," he whispered. Rutherford nodded, his head bowed. "But they will be avenged, I promise you that." Rutherford wiped his eyes and sat up straight, the comment returning his resolve.

"Anything I can do to help right now?" Rutherford asked.

"I think we have it under control for now," James said smiling at him. "If you want to grab a nap for a couple hours before we start the interrogation I don't think anyone would fault you. You did good work today, you should take a break."

Rutherford was suddenly very tired. He stood up and stretched. "Ok, I will be in the locker room if anyone is looking for me," he said. "Seriously though, don't let me sleep too long, I want to be a part of this."

With their assurances that they would wake him before any major undertaking, Rutherford walked off to get some much needed sleep. Mac returned and took a seat again.

"Rutherford was in charge of the shift when it got hit," James said to Mac and Seth. "He is the one who shot the other asshole in the lockup right now, right as the guy was setting up to ambush civilians at the mall. He's a good man, but this is going to bother him when all is said and done."

"No doubt," said Mac. "It would bother me too. The more he can be a part of the follow-up the better I would think though."

"Definitely," said James. "We can have him in on the interrogations. He has no issue with our enhanced techniques."

"I doubt we will need enhanced techniques anymore," said Seth. "These two are done, they will tell us anything we want to know."

56.

Marie had left the television off for a couple of days. She felt safe on the ranch, and so far removed from everything else that it didn't seem to matter much. She had returned to her normal homeschooling schedule with the kids, who for their part didn't ask any more questions about the attack and seemed to have mostly forgotten it ever happened. She looked at the kids and smiled, wishing she had some of the resiliency that their youth provides. For her, the attack was still raw in her mind, and she tried hard to push it out.

"Where's Dad?" her youngest daughter asked. Sarah was the closest of the children with her father, too young to remember the arguing and leaving the way the older kids did.

"He's working, honey," Marie answered, moving a long, curly lock of hair from the front of Sarah's face and tucking it behind her ear.

Marie knew that Ray would be involved in whatever was going on. She no longer loved him, not in the way she once had, but the two were still parents to their children and she considered him a friend of sorts now. It was a strange way to consider their relationship, but their relationship was strange. Whatever was going on, Marie hoped that he was safe but knew that he rarely considered his own safety in such matters. She was consoled with the fact that she knew that Ray was good at what he did. Whether it was intellectual or actual physical skills, Ray was good at it. She hoped for now that he was only using his intellectual skills, but assumed that at some point he would join the fight if there was one to join.

Her phone rang as she considered the possibilities and she saw that it was Ray calling.

"Hello?" she said upon answering.

"Hey, how are you and the kids doing?" Ray asked.

"Everyone's good, they seem relaxed and have not mentioned it for a day or two now," she said.

"Ok, good," he replied. "I think we are out of the woods for now, there is no intelligence that would suggest another attack is coming, so you can probably resume normal activities."

"Thanks," Marie said. "I don't know if I even know what normal activities are anymore, Ray."

"Are you ok?" he asked. "I know that was a pretty big deal." He still hadn't told her about the shooting he was involved in, deciding he probably never would.

"I think so," she said. "It just scares me to think of what could have happened with the kids."

"I know," he replied. "You did good, that should make you feel better."

"Thanks," she said. "I am doing schoolwork with them right now, did you need something?"

"No, not at all," he said. "Just checking in on you guys to make sure you are ok. I will talk to you soon."

"Sounds good," Marie said before disconnecting. She looked at her daughter. "That was your Dad, he is doing just fine." The little girl smiled at her and skipped off to the kitchen.

57

Grace looked at Ray and hesitated for a minute before asking, "Are you up for a road trip, Ray?"

"Where to?" Ray asked. It didn't really matter where it was to, Ray was pleased at the thought of some time alone driving with Grace.

"Amarillo," Grace said. "We have some intelligence units in place there that it might be good to meet up with. They have some information they want to share in person."

As they headed north on 35, Ray looked over at Grace who was flipping through some papers on her lap.

"Do we think that the Austin rebellion was tied to the attacks form California?" he asked her.

She looked up from her papers at him. "We don't know, but the timing cannot be coincidental. There are two theories right now. One being that it was a coordinated part of the attacks. The other that California launched the attack around the rebellion without actually coordinating with them," she spoke calmly and thoughtfully. "The mayor and the city board are not answering questions right now, and we are holding off on using enhance interrogation techniques at the moment."

"The reason I ask is that if it was a coordinated effort, we should probably start rounding up the rebels in Austin as enemy combatants," Ray said. "If they are coordinating, then that leaves a large insurgency group in place in Austin right now."

"Yes, good point," she nodded. "Do *you* think they are related?"

"I don't get that feeling," Ray said. "I think California capitalized on the chaos in Austin, and there is no doubt that they share similar political beliefs, but I don't think that Austin was actually a part of the attack. If it were, those buses would have already been in place in Austin, not still on their way. The military hardware they were carrying would have made that a very different scene," he shuddered as he thought of that possibility.

"I think that as well," Grace said. "I would hate to start a round-up there if we don't have to. They took such a beating the last couple days that I think they will lay low if they aren't bothered, the Resistance that is."

Grace and Ray spoke more casually during the rest of the trip to Amarillo. Grace inquired more about Ray's family and Ray answered candidly as always. Despite being the Attorney General of the state, the youngest ever elected, she was not at all arrogant. She and Ray were talking as though they had known each other for years, and they trusted one another completely.

Ray knew he was in dangerous territory with Grace. She was not only beautiful, but also intelligent. He knew he could quickly fall for her and he genuinely did not want to. The last thing he needed right now was a new relationship. He was just starting to get to a point where his kids were comfortable around him, at least the ones he had with Marie, and he wanted to keep working on those relationships. He had no time or energy for a new relationship with a woman. And yet, there was Grace sitting next to him in the car, her green eyes shining brilliantly with an intense intellect and compassion, asking for nothing from him but offering so much.

He reminded himself that there was nothing more than a working relationship with her right now, that she had said or done nothing to indicate she was even interested in anything more than that. Ray was suddenly embarrassed by his own arrogance. Why should he think that there would be more, that she would want anything more than the working relationship that they had right now. She was out of his league anyway. The fact that they were becoming friends did not mean she was interested in anything more. Ray comforted himself with that fact, and resolved not to worry about it anymore. She was a good friend to have.

"Ray," Grace looked over at him, "what do you think about a high profile, state initiated response?"

"I thought that was what the assassination was," Ray said, meeting her gaze.

"That was not state initiated, there is nothing to tie us to that," she replied. "I am talking about something like you and I discussed before, something obviously officially done by the state but we don't acknowledge it."

"Yes, I think that is totally appropriate as we have already discussed," Ray said. "But having said that, hitting the Speaker of the State Assembly is a pretty big deal, anything more might escalate the situation significantly."

"Escalate it to what?" Grace inquired.

"War," Ray said, pausing to look her in the eye again.

"We're at war already," Grace said. "It is not a matter of escalating the war but of achieving the greatest effect."

"Good point," Ray said. "They started this war, I suppose there isn't much we could do that would escalate it with them. I am more concerned with the war expanding, with other states entering the situation or even the federal government," he explained. "That being said, I think a carefully selected official response, combined with a lack of comment, would be appropriate."

"Infrastructure or leadership?" Grace asked.

Ray paused. "You mean destroying infrastructure or further targeted assassinations?"

"Yes, or both?" Grace replied without emotion.

"I think that depends completely on your goal," Ray said. "Destroying infrastructure sends a punitive message and also limits their ability to strike us again, which justifies it. Taking out leadership send a different kind of message."

"What kind of message does it send?" Grace asked.

Ray looked down at his forearm, the tattoo covered by his sleeve. "Don't tread on me."

58.

"We have Grace and Ray on their way to Amarillo to meet with you, Mac," Clark said over the landline. "You know who Grace is, and Ray is a good guy, you will like him. Former cop, works on policy now. He has been in line with our response from the beginning, and helped smooth it out some. The idea for uploading the video confessions, that was his idea in theory, though he does not know that."

"He is clear to speak freely around then?" Mac asked.

"Absolutely, same as if you were talking to me or James. We'll talk soon," Clark said before hanging up.

Capo and Adam had been fed and were sleeping soundly. Mac, James, and Seth walked the halls of the police station to stretch a bit. The mood there was somber. Fourteen members of this family were dead, nothing would bring them back and no amount of response would heal the loss for the remaining officers. Seth felt this more than the others. As a former police officer, he understood the culture which, while similar to the military, was still different. War was a part of life for the military, not that the pain of loss was less when a soldier falls, but it is not completely unexpected in the grand scheme of things. Police officers were not supposed to be killed. It happens sometimes, but it is rare and always unexpected. Having nearly an entire patrol shift wiped out is unimaginable. The people in this building were reeling from that pain and adjusting to a new reality. This tragedy would change Amarillo Police Department forever. How it would change would be up to them.

Chief Bradley Hughes had spent almost all of the past few days dealing with press and with the city administration to lead the clean-up and rebuilding of city infrastructure. He had spent almost no time at all in the police station, but he was there now. He walked slowly down the hall, stopping at each office to speak with whoever was in there. The cup of coffee in his hand had gone cold a long while ago.

"Good morning, Chief," Mac said as they approached him.

"Good morning, fellas," Chief Bradley smiled warmly, his eyes red and swollen.

"How are you holding up?" James asked.

"As well as can be, given the circumstances," he said. Brad looked around at the three men in front of him and smiled. These were the men that would avenge his officers, he could feel it radiating from them like heat from a light bulb. "Have you men had lunch yet?"

"Not yet, sir," Seth answered.

"Come on in to my office, I have food there and a table we can talk at," he waved for them to follow him.

Brad's office was nicely appointed, a large wooden desk and two massive bookshelves were on one wall. The middle of the large room was filled by a dark wooden conference table with room for eight people. A brown leather couch completed the high quality furnishings. Outside of the books that filled the bookshelves, and the furniture itself, the room was relatively minimalist in nature. There were no pictures on the chief's desk, no artwork on the walls. All three men had their gaze attracted to the two rifles resting against the desk in an upright position. One was a full-size AR-15 with standard carry handle sights. A basic weapon, in the basic configuration. The second was Remington 700 bolt action rifle with a scope and bi-pod.

"Were you a sniper, Chief?" Seth asked upon seeing the rifle.

"I was the team leader for our sniper element on the SWAT team years ago," Brad replied. "Seems like a lifetime ago. Those are always sitting by my desk in case I need to run out to help my people on the street."

"Good man," Seth smiled. In his experience, most chiefs were politicians. This one was still a warrior.

"I was in Las Vegas at a conference when this happened," he said, eyes beginning to water. "Those didn't do me much good on the day I needed them most, the day I needed to be here most."

"Don't beat yourself up over this, Chief," James said. "Those teams had every advantage, one more guy with a rifle would not have changed the outcome. You have the rest of your life to make sure this never happens again, but there is *nothing* you could have done to stop it or to change the outcome."

Brad looked up gratefully, "thank you, I needed to hear that." He took a sip of his cold coffee and grabbed a pot of fresh coffee and cups from his secretary's office just outside his door. He poured coffee for the three men and offered creamers and sugar that none accepted. The coffee was good. Brad regularly brought in the freshly ground beans from a specialty store down the road. A Texas pecan dark roast blend that was really better with a little cream and sugar, but Brad understood why the trio took their coffee black. Cream and sugar wasn't always available in their line of work, getting used to drinking it black was a safe bet.

"Do you have what you need here, is there anything I can get you?" Brad asked, looking to James.

"You and your people have been excellent, Chief," James smiled at him. "We have everything we need. Could we possibly use a room for a videotaped interrogation, though? Something not immediately recognizable as a police station, preferably something we could sterilize for visual and sound to prevent anyone from identifying it?"

"Of course, we have an interrogation room already wired for video and audio, we can put white sheets and sound deadening panels in there within the hour," he nodded. "Will that work?"

"Perfectly," James smiled, and took another sip of his coffee.

59.

Ray and Grace pulled into the driveway of the secure parking garage and waited to be buzzed through the gate. The drive had been long, nearly four hours, and both were anxious to stretch their legs. Ray dropped Grace off at the door and then parked the car. He jogged over to where she waited for him and they were let inside by an Amarillo officer who led them to the Chief's office. There they found all four men seated at the table. They all rose to their feet as Grace walked in.

"Good afternoon, gentlemen," she smiled and put a file of papers down on the conference table.

"Afternoon, ma'am," each replied at once.

"Thank you for allowing us the use of your facility, Chief," Grace said to Brad. "I am so sorry for your loss."

"Thank you, and you are very welcome," he replied somberly.

As Grace took a seat, everyone sat back down. Ray sat next to Seth.

"Everyone, this is Ray Tucker," Grace introduced him to the group. "He is a consultant with the Administration on special incidents." Ray glanced over at her, wondering if she had come up with that title on the fly or if she had thought about it before. "He is also a retired cop, I know that means something to some of you," she smiled.

Ray shook hands around the room. As he reached for Seth's hand, Seth looked him in the eye and said, "Welcome, brother." Ray smiled and nodded. He felt at home with these men. And this kind of work, with these kind of people, made him feel alive again.

"We are about ready to start our interrogation," James said. "Chief here was kind enough to sterilize a room and allow us use of his recording equipment, which is top level stuff. Ray, what is your experience with interviews and interrogations?"

"Well, I was a detective for ten years of my career in law enforcement," Ray said. "I'm comfortable if that's what you're asking."

"We would like you to do the questioning for this one then," James said. "You know what the whole story needs to look like. We will have them both in the room together, almost like a panel, and let them string all of the information together. We can edit the video afterward for release, but there are no rules here, Ray. You're not a cop interviewing a criminal. These are enemy combatants, terrorists. Use that as you see fit."

Ray borrowed a legal pad from Grace's stack, and a pen from the chief's desk and began outlining the interview. He worked out loud, and the rest of the people in the room gathered around him to see what his plan was.

"I want to completely implicate Dante Malone in this from the beginning," Ray began. "I want them to discuss The Resistance and the ideology in detail, why they joined, all of that. After that, I will have them discuss the training for the attacks, and the planning. We will also discuss the professor and the bio attack plan. I want Capo to explain the financing of the operation, how much of it was official state funds and so on. Finally, I want them to discuss anything they know about future attacks in the works."

"Who do you want in the room with you?" James asked.

"I'm fine by myself," he said. "We can change that up if needed, but let's start with just me. Someone outside the door and the rest monitoring the equipment should be good."

"I'll hang outside the door," Seth said. He liked working with another cop again, and was eager to play the role of back-up.

The group left Brad's office and went to the interrogation room where the crew had just finished sterilizing the set. They explained to Ray where he would be off camera, a table and chairs were covered by a white tarp and were placed to position Capo and Adam in full view of the camera. White sheeting covered all of the walls and behind that were the sound deadening panels. It would be very difficult to get any clues as to a location by watching anything recorded in the room. The group left for a moment, and then James and Mac returned with Capo and Adam, sat them in their assigned seats and left the room. Ray stood leaning against the wall, looking at them emotionlessly.

"Hello, sir," Capo volunteered. Unlike Adam, he did not appear outwardly scared.

Ray did not answer, just looked at him directly in the eyes.

"Sir, we've been talking, and, and, whatever you want to know we will tell you," Adam said as Capo nodded.

Ray stood up straight. "That's good, the easier you make this the better," he said. "I believe in working smarter, not harder, so less you make me work the better it will be for both of you. But let's be clear, this is not a criminal interrogation and I am not a cop. You have no rights. This will be painful for you if you are uncooperative, I assure you of that."

Both men nodded, Adam swallowed hard. Ray began the interview allowing both men plenty of time to talk. Unlike the video confessions aired on television the other night, this was a long narrative with both men allowed the freedom to talk. Ray guided the discussion according to the outline he had written earlier, but the men filled in all of the details remarkably well. Details that Capo knew well, such as Dante Malone's role in the attacks, were discussed by him. Adam was more familiar with the inner workings of The Resistance and explained the movement's profile, philosophy, and role in the attacks. After about an hour and a half, Ray asked a few specific questions.

"How did Dante Malone, the Governor of California, pay for the attacks?" he asked.

"Well, he allowed me complete control over the base spending and said to get The Resistance whatever it needed," Capo answered.

"The buses?" Ray asked.

"Yes, I bought the buses with Guard funds, used Guard mechanics to customize and armor them," he replied.

"Weapons?" Ray asked.

"All Guard weapons, except for some that the group personally owned, which were not many," he replied.

"The professor and the bio attack, how many more are there like him?" Ray asked.

"Stevens is the only one I worked with," Capo began but was interrupted by Adam.

"There are two others somewhere in New York, at least that's what I heard," Adam said.

Capo looked at him, this was the first he had ever heard of a part of the attack plan being outside of California.

"Where, who, and what?" Ray prompted.

"I don't know," Adam responded, visibly nervous, "I just heard a couple of the team members talking about it one night. They didn't say any more than that. Just that there was a biological project underway in two cities in New York. I don't know if they meant building weapons there or planning attacks."

"Was New York an intended target?" Ray asked.

"Of course not, they are natural allies of The Resistance," Adam said, more comfortable in his understanding of the group than in specific planning details which he had not ever really been involved in.

"So, New York locations may be developing or storing bioweapons for use in future attacks by The Resistance? Is that fair to say?" Ray paraphrased.

"For sure, but I don't know where or how much," Adam said.

Capo was quiet during this part of the discussion, his involvement with this movement was mostly limited to the state level operations. He had not involved himself in the intricacies of The Resistance other than giving the members equipment and training. Most of the planning had been done by them to give him and the Governor deniability. A New York connection to bioweapons was news to him as well. He had been the liaison to Professor Stevens, but had assumed the anthrax aerosol attack would be a one-time event meant to crush the spirit of Texans, not a prolonged engagement strategy.

"Capo," Ray's attention turned to him, "where is Dante Malone's hideaway, his bunker?"

"Lake Tahoe," he answered without hesitation. "Not really a bunker, I mean, it is a sturdy house but it is just a house. It is very remote though, that is where its safety lies."

"Do you know exactly where it is?" Ray asked.

"Of course," Capo said proudly, "I was part of his evacuation team."

"You will show us on a map then?" Ray asked.

"I will do better than that, my friend," Capo chuckled, "I have the GPS coordinates memorized."

60.

Dante tried to reach Tim Leland's office using a secure phone in the Chevrolet Suburban that he was travelling in as part of the caravan on its way to Lake Tahoe. The three black vehicles travelled in excess of 90 miles per hour with their emergency lights activated. The front vehicle contained six security personnel. The middle vehicle was only himself and Julie Taylor, his chief of staff. The trailing vehicle held eight security team members as a "jump out" unit.

Julie was crying silently. She had only a small bag of personal items with her. Julie was intentionally left out of all discussions surrounding the attacks or The Resistance and did what she did best, ran the governor's office and the politics surrounding it. She knew nothing of what had occurred, and was reluctant to believe what was becoming abundantly clear in the face of developing evidence.

"Please tell me we were not involved in those horrible attacks on Texas," she said without looking at Dante.

"If that is what you want to hear," Dante said condescendingly, "then we were not involved in those horrible attacks on Texas."

"Dante, how could we have done that?" she pleaded with tears in her eyes.

"Julie, you are an excellent chief of staff," Dante said. "But this is something altogether different, something you didn't need to know about. And judging from your current reaction, that was the right call."

The convoy weaved through traffic, taking the shoulder where needed to avoid any delays. Julie sat staring out the window, less afraid for her own personal safety than Dante was. Her greatest emotion right now was sorrow. She thought of the innocent people that had died in the bombings and shootings less than a full week ago, the police officers who would not return to their families, and her sorrow shifted toward guilt. She blamed herself for not seeing any signs that this was going to occur, and wracked her mind to think of something that would have indicated it was a possibility. She could think of none, other than Dante's personal affection for the group that called itself The Resistance. That alone was not enough to predict he would be part of a terrorist attack on another state, was it?

There was snow on the ground when they arrived at the remote house in Lake Tahoe. The outbuildings were for the security teams, and the K9 team had arrived just before the convoy. Dante waited patiently in the Suburban as he watched the dogs work the exterior and interior of the property, sniffing for bombs. Dante was more of a cat person, but he saw the value in these particular dogs and had appreciation for them accordingly. He just did not want them in the house while he was in it.

He looked around at the wooded and snow covered property, at the mountains in the background, and thought it was a pretty place to live. He preferred the city, of course, but this was not an unhappy place. Circumstances aside, he would be comfortable here for as long as he needed to be. The secure satellite links were in place and he would be very difficult to find. Only his security team even knew the place existed, he had paid for it with his own private funds and placed it in a trust to avoid public knowledge of its location or ownership. Having needed to use it for security now, he was already deciding on how to have the State reimburse all of his expenses once this was over. He was pretty sure he could get the State to pay for the whole place for him, he would have to think about that angle. Even hiding could be profitable if one worked it the right way.

Julie got out of the vehicle without saying anything and walked to the house with her purse and small duffle bag. Inside she found a decanter of scotch on a small cart in the hallway and poured herself a glass using one of the tumblers on the cart. Taking a large sip, she winced at the burn for a moment and then walked to the bedroom on the left side of the hallway. She placed the glass on the dresser and removed the bottle of sleeping pills she had been using the past several days to help her rest. There looked to be about fifteen or so pills left in the bottle. She poured them all into her mouth and took another large swig of scotch and swallowed hard. Wincing again at the burn she paused before finishing off the rest of the glass. Julie looked up toward Heaven and whispered, "I am so sorry." She took off her shoes, laid down on the bed, and closed her eyes.

61.

Austin had devolved into something out of an apocalyptic western movie. The police were mostly gone, the few that remained had no control over anything that was occurring. DPS troopers were patrolling where they could, but between security at the Governor's mansion and the events around the state, they had very little personnel to spare. They were simply responding to in-progress violent emergencies when they could, anything with a lower priority went unanswered.

In the vacuum left by the lack of police was filled by several groups of local militias. They were not affiliated with the Hill Country Militia and were far less organized. The groups were settling into a routine of hunting down the progressive groups and killing them in the streets. It was dangerous to wear a black hoodie, it was deadly to wear one with an anarchist symbol on it. The militias were purging the city of the leftist activists at the barrel of a gun.

The car bomb and shootout at the Governor's mansion had been more than most of the progressive groups had bargained for, and most of the activists proved far less committed to the cause than their rhetoric leading up to the event had suggested. Most of the activists gave up and went back to their normal lives. Those that did not, those that still proudly covered their faces and took to the streets were promptly met with deadly force. The actual number of shootings and extrajudicial executions that had occurred could not properly be counted, and probably never would be. Many of the bodies had been unceremoniously dumped into the Colorado River. Others ended up in dumpsters. A particularly eerie and gruesome mass funeral pyre had been held at Zilker Park, where an estimated two hundred bodies were 'cremated.' Even more of the bodies were still where they fell, in streets and allies and parking lots.

"Tim," Jack said after hanging up his cell phone, "the situation here in Austin is tenuous at best. These militias are basically doing a purge of the leftists."

"I heard," Tim said. "Honestly, I don't know that that is the worst thing right now."

"I don't have enough people to effectively police this city right now, do you think we just let them police themselves for now and reign it in once we lift the martial law status?" Jack asked.

"That's exactly what I think we should do," Tim said. "The Left started this mess, they are getting their just desserts at this point. I am not talking about murdering folks, but this is righteous warfare at this point, Jack."

"I agree," Jack said. With a little gallows humor, he added, "Place was due for a bit of a purge anyway. Good to thin the herd now and then."

Tim laughed at his friend and poured each of them a drink. They sipped bourbon in silence for a few minutes.

"Grace and Clark are working on the last part of this response, Jack," Tim said.

"I know, any word from them yet?" Jack asked.

"No, they told me they would have a package to me shortly," he replied. "You know, this administration is so like-minded that I have had very little stress during this whole incident, all things considered. You, Clark, Grace, this guy Ray. All of you seem to be thinking the same way I am. It is very consoling."

"It's easy with the right leadership," Jack said and raised his glass toward Tim. "You have handled yourself well here, Tim. No one has doubted you or your resolve for one second here."

"Thank you, sincerely," Tim said. "Let me ask you, what do you think is next? I mean, are we going to war with California? What does that even look like?"

"I don't know, Tim. I think we take it one step at a time and see where it all leads," Jack said.

"I mean, seriously. I have my Guard generals drawing up actual battle plans, occupation scenarios for attacking and conquering another state. This is almost too surreal," Tim took another sip of the bourbon.

"I don't think the occupation scenarios are realistic," Jack said. "It is good to be prepared, but I think the feds will get involved at some point, maybe not until after we kick California's ass though," he chuckled.

"I am praying it does not get to that point," Tim said.

62.

Dave called Ray to tell him that the Foundation's building had burned down, probably shortly after the beginning of all of the events had unfolded. Until things stabilized in Austin and they could rebuild, everyone would be working remotely. Dave didn't ask Ray for an update on what he was doing, he understood that there must be confidentiality in the consulting work he was undertaking. He simply wished him well and said they would talk again soon. Ray didn't ask about the body of the man he had shot in the lobby, he assumed it had been incinerated in the blaze.

Ray hung up his phone and went into the room where the rest of the team was replaying the interview and editing a video for public release. The IT manager for Amarillo was helping to edit the video and proved to be very good at this kind of work. The final product flowed well, implicating California as a state and Dante Malone specifically in the attacks. Sensitive information was edited out, such as the whereabouts of Malone's hideout. Ray made sure to compliment the manager and thank him for his efforts. He remembered the thankless work performed by the IT workers at his former police department, how they were rarely recognized for the work they did.

The video would be uploaded by the Hill County Militia under the same fictitious account they used for the first releases, leaving the connection to Texas as a state undetected even if they were eventually uncovered as having posted it. The public opinion campaign that the first confession videos represented had been very effective. Leftists argued that Texas deserved what it got and more, but moderates and conservatives were outraged that a state could have been involved in such an atrocity. Even the generally left of center news media seemed appalled by the revelations, and all were reporting that Governor Malone was nowhere to be found for comment.

"Liberty Policy Foundation burned down," Ray whispered to Grace.

"Ray, I'm so sorry," she said looking at him with her soft green eyes.

"It's insured, not that big a deal I suppose," he said. "Just surprised me a little is all. That building was historic, I hope they can replicate it."

"When?" she asked.

"Not sure, but I am assuming it was the first day all this went down, they had covered the lobby in gasoline when we made our retreat" he said. "That was obviously their intention from the start." Ray wanted to tell her about what happened in the lobby, but he really had not fully processed it himself and didn't want to say anything he shouldn't. It began to occur to him that he might not ever talk about it all, just another event to tuck away in a compartment in his mind.

"I had no idea you were in the middle of all this when it broke loose," she whispered. "I spoke to Jack on the phone earlier," Grace said, leaning in toward him, "it sounds like Austin is turning into the Wild West right now. Militia groups are hunting down the progressives and anarchists, there are no cops left there to referee it."

Ray took the opportunity to lean closer to her as well, feeling a little sheepish given that they were not talking about anything particularly private or sensitive. "That doesn't surprise me, I bet a lot of Texans down there are jumping at the opportunity to take back the city from the leftwing mob that controlled it."

"It is more than just occupying or controlling the area though, Ray," Grace said. "There is a lot of killing going on, it is more like a purge than anything else."

"Grace, if this whole thing breaks out into a war between the states, even just the states of Texas and California," Ray said softly, "that kind of purge will happen all over Texas. This will be the most dangerous place in the world for a liberal or a progressive to be."

"Do you think so?" Grace asked, somewhat alarmed.

"I do," Ray nodded. "I think that some groups will take advantage of the chaos and the fog of war and use it to rid the state of anyone they don't agree with," Ray said. "The possible war that we have brewing here would be just as dangerous from internal threats as it would from whoever we are fighting outside the Texas borders. The news media will be unable to bring attention to the violence because they will be unwelcome here as well, no one will differentiate them from the leftwing activists, something they have brought upon themselves. Constant coverage of leftwing mobs running conservatives out of restaurants or preventing them from public speaking has agitated many on the right, they are going to welcome this fight."

Grace jotted down some notes on her legal pad. "I genuinely had not thought of that."

The team huddled around the television to watch the final version of the video. It was edited down to about eight minutes, all were pleased with the message it sent. Mac took the flash drive and went out to upload the video from his own encrypted laptop under a fictitious account. He emailed all the major news networks with a copy. The video went viral within the hour.

63.

"The House just passed a bill dissolving the city of Austin and making it into a district of the capitol, similar to Washington DC," Clark told Tim over the phone. "The Senate is going to pass the bill today, should be on your desk by this afternoon."

"Ok, good," Tim said, "did Grace look over it yet?"

"She wrote it," Clark chuckled.

"Of course, what was I thinking?" Tim laughed.

"The Mayor will be appointed by you with Senate confirmation, and a subcommittee in the House will act as the City board," Clark said. "There is a two-year sunset provision, in case this does not work out as well as we hope it will."

"Very good, and that video was excellent, Clark," Tim said. "All of the national news coverage is critical of California right now, even the progressives are saying this was out of line."

"Yes, public opinion is definitely in our favor," Clark said. "We'll see how that plays out with the coming responses, though."

"I don't much care either way," Tim said. "Texas will always be Texas, we will always defend ourselves and punch back when we are hit."

"Agreed," said Clark. "Any coverage of the Speaker's death in California that you have seen? I have only seen a couple of short articles on it, nothing tying it to what happened here."

"I haven't seen anything on it, the confession videos are sucking all the air out of the room I think," Tim said.

Clark hung up the phone and sat at the table with Ray and Grace. Grace was on her laptop typing away furiously, Ray was looking at news coverage of the events. He noted that there was not yet any comprehensive coverage of all of the events, that the media was jumping from event to event and not connecting the overall picture very well. This could be intentional, or just incompetent, Ray wasn't sure which. The last video did most of that work for the media anyway, which might be why they were content just focusing on individual events.

He did note one article in a conservative blog that made mention of trying to locate the origin of the videos, that they came under the same user profile, but attempts at identification were unsuccessful. Ray was impressed with the level at which Mac's operation was able to remain under the radar. Ray had never even heard of the group before all of this happened. If he had, there was a good chance he would have tried to join them, but he assumed this was by invitation only. Grace paused in her typing and Ray looked over at her.

"Even with an obvious response by Texas, our media plan is to neither confirm nor deny anything, right?" she asked him.

"That is my recommendation," Ray said, "the official policy is of course up to the Governor."

"Of course, but that is what you recommend?" she smiled.

"Yes," Ray said. "How will we respond to the feds if they ask? What about the President?"

"Same way," Grace said. "Until we are forced to say anything, we won't."

"Forced...that is a whole new scenario," Ray smiled.

"Let's hope not," Grace said.

"We have a couple of members of our anti-terror team from DPS in Washington right now briefing the President's staff on what happened," Clark said. "We are pretty sure they will give us some space to do what we need to, at least for a while."

"Are they briefing the President on our anticipated response?" Ray asked.

"No," Clark hesitated, "not yet."

"Any follow-up on the New York info we got from Adam?" Ray asked.

"Jack has been notified, we are keeping it from the FBI for now," Clark said. "Jack will let us know if his people need any help." Clark tapped his pen on the table thoughtfully. "I am glad we beefed up the anti-terror unit last budget," Clark smiled.

Ray paused to consider what the New York piece might mean. He did not say anything out loud because there was enough to consider without the added possibilities he was playing out in his mind. If the New York connections were simply scientists like Professor Stevens then the whole thing would be relatively simple. If, however, New York were more broadly involved then the scenario would be very different. For now, Ray would assume that the New York issue was an unfortunately located extension of the California attack and that the individuals involved were isolated. There was enough to consider right now, the rest could wait on whatever the anti-terror teams would discover.

Mac and Seth came in to the room to say goodbye.

"Where are you guys heading?" Ray asked as he shook hands with Mac.

"New York," he said with a wink.

64.

The following evening everyone met at the governor's mansion in Tim's office. The bill dissolving Austin as a city had been signed earlier that morning, effective immediately. Grace passed out a packet of papers to everyone at the table. Ray flipped through the booklet as she began speaking.

"Governor, we have compiled a report for you detailing what we know up to this point, and what our responses have been," she said. "I will let everyone look through this tonight but ask that you pay special attention to the last two chapters which include our possible state responses and the New York contingency plans."

Ray looked up at her, a little surprised. They had not discussed that last part together, and now he was interested to see what her take on it was. Thus far, she and Clark had been able to put together the same ideas and the same plans that he would have. He was not upset at being excluded, but it made his mind drift to areas he might be more useful in if they had the policy angle handled. His mind was traveling to New York with the militia. He pulled it back into the room while Grace finished the briefing with the Governor.

"Thank you, Grace," Tim said. "I think we should all get some rest tonight and read through this. Let's have a discussion tomorrow morning about the next steps."

The group all retired to different guest rooms in the mansion. Ray took his boots off and changed into a pair of gym shorts and a t-shirt, his usual sleeping attire. He poured some bourbon into a glass from the bar in the room and sat atop the blankets reading the last two chapters of the report. He skipped ahead with the understanding that he probably knew most of the historical background, having written much of it himself. Ray took a sip and looked at the list of locations for possible airstrikes detailing potential casualties and damage predictions.

He was not surprised that this was a possible response, after all he had made it a part of his recommendations, but it was the one most likely to have complications. Having Texas warplanes hit targets in California was not only dangerous but difficult to deny. As he had recommended, the plan would not be to deny the strikes, just not to comment or claim responsibility. It was the riskiest of the recommendations and he was suddenly unsure he should have made it.

When Ray had been on the SWAT team during his time as a cop, he had planned several search warrant raids. Each time, without fail, he had questioned himself about the plan. He knew that if one of his men was injured or killed he would blame himself for overlooking something in the planning. During the ride in the van to one of his last raids, he was staring down at the rifle propped between his knees, contemplating the plans that would be violently executed in a few minutes. A teammate next to him patted him on the shoulder and Ray looked up to see his teammate's big smile. It was a crazy look, but it made Ray realize that all of these men would not want to be anywhere else in the world right now. They were ready, this was their calling, and they loved it.

Ray understood in that moment that no matter what happened, they would not blame him. Quite to the contrary, they were grateful for the opportunity to be there and would not miss it for the world. It was one of many moments when he realized how lucky he was to be among such men and women, and he was grateful to have been a part of their lives. It was also what he missed most about the profession. There was an irrevocable loyalty to one another. There were officers on his agency that he didn't particular care for, maybe one or two that he downright disliked, but he would have killed or died for any of them regardless. That included the ones he didn't like. That kind of loyalty and commitment was something Ray had yet to find outside of law enforcement. But this was different. The people who could be affected by this plan, a plan he was at least partially responsible for, didn't sign up for any of this.

He took another sip and looked up at the ceiling, exhaling slowly. A soft knock at the door got his attention and he sat upright. He glanced at the gun on the nightstand next to him, then tucked it under the pillow before going to the door.

When he opened it, there was Grace holding her packet. She was barefoot, wearing a sweatshirt and yoga pants, and she looked adorable. Her casual look was even more appealing than the sharp business dress that Ray was used to seeing her in.

"Got a minute?" she asked.

"Of course, come on in," he said. "Want a drink?"

"Brought one," she laughed. Ray noticed she had a glass of bourbon in her hand as well. He was shamefully cognizant that the yoga pants had taken his attention away from her hands. So much for being a highly trained police officer.

Grace sat down at the small table in the room and Ray picked up his packet and sat across from her. The lighting in the room accented the reddish tints in her hair, perfectly contrasting them with the emerald qualities of her eyes.

"Nice tattoo," she said as Ray reached for his drink, the coiled snake on his forearm visible for the first time since they had known each other.

"Thank you," he smiled, "youthful indiscretion."

"Have you always been a conservative?" she asked.

"Yes, I can't remember a time that I wasn't," he replied. "I was in first grade when a teacher came into our classroom, out of breath, and told us that President Reagan had been shot. She was almost in tears, we all were. I suppose that shaped some of my conservatism, just my association of it with him. No other political philosophy ever interested me after that. So, first grade, I guess. How about you?"

"Well," she smiled, "I wasn't born yet when Reagan was shot." She swirled the bourbon in her glass, bringing it close to her nose to savor the smell before she took a sip. Ray noticed that she did not even flinch. "I was probably a liberal for the most part until law school."

"Really?" Ray smiled. "I thought law school turned people into liberals, not the other way around."

"I had an awesome teacher in my first semester," she said. "He was a former cop, and his views on Constitutional Law opened my eyes." She looked at him and smiled. "You remind me of him."

"I'm flattered," he grinned, taking another sip.

"May I?" she asked, pointing to his arm. Ray moved his arm toward her and she took his wrist with one hand, then traced the snake with the tip of her index finger. The dark gray nail polish on her fingernails matched that on her toes. Ray would have more comfortable with the shock of a tazer than what he was feeling right now. "This is nice work, who did it?"

"Uh, a friend of mine back up north," he tried not to stutter. "He was a cop that ran a tattoo shop on the side. What's on your mind, Grace?"

"I was trying to go to sleep and couldn't" she said, suddenly aware she might be intruding, "but I can go if you are busy or want to be alone."

"No, no, not at all," he said, reassuring her that she was always welcome around him. "I was reading through your packet, I am glad you came over."

"What do you think of it?" she asked.

"It's fantastic," he said. He took another sip and then asked, "Grace, are you sure you guys need me here?"

"You have been a huge help, Ray," she said. "Why would you ask that? Are you wanting to leave?"

"Not at all," he said quickly, "this has been an honor to work with you and the rest of the team. I am just wondering if I might be more useful elsewhere. You and Clark are sharp people, and most of what I have advised you has already been thought through by the two of you before I say it."

"Thank you for saying so, but that's not entirely true," she said, smiling at him. "You have been more helpful than you know. Is there something else, I am gathering that is not the only reason you would contemplate leaving?"

Ray leaned back in the chair a little, taking a sip of the bourbon. He looked at her and was keenly aware that her beautiful green eyes were reading his face, gathering the information that was unspoken. "I have missed being a cop on the street since the day I retired," he said. "I would not mind being part of this in a different capacity."

"You mean with the militia, or with the anti-terror team?" she looked at him sincerely.

"Either," he said.

"I know that you would be welcome on either," she said, "but we could really use you here."

"Ok, no problem at all," he said sitting up a little. "I just want to make sure that I am being useful wherever I am at, I will serve in any capacity you see fit to use me in."

"Ray, you are being useful, but if you need to be a part of the action everyone here will understand that," she said. "Especially the governor and Jack, they were cops too."

"No, no," he said, "I am ok doing this so long as I am helping." As he spoke, Ray realized that staying in this position meant daily contact with Grace, something he would never complain about.

"It's getting late, I should probably be getting back to bed," she said as she stood up.

Ray didn't want her to leave, but also knew she should. "We do have an early day tomorrow," he nodded.

She walked toward the door and Ray followed her, opening it for her as she began to leave. She stopped suddenly and turned around, kissing Ray on his cheek, her breath warm on his face. "Good night," she whispered and walked out without looking back. Ray watched her walk back to her room, the yoga pants complimenting her athletic form.

Ray returned to the bed, his face warm. Unsure if it was the bourbon or the kiss, he assumed it to be the latter. He considered now the real possibility that Grace might be interested in a relationship. Then again, maybe Grace had just had a little too much bourbon tonight and tomorrow this would all be forgotten. Ray allowed himself to consider what it would mean to be in a relationship again and was torn. There was no part of him that wanted to go back to his previous marriage or the life that either of his marriages had been for him. At the same time, there was no denying that he was amazed by Grace and that he was unavoidably attracted to her. Ray's mind lingered on her kiss momentarily, and then he pushed all of it into a compartment, turned out the light on the nightstand, and went to sleep.

65.

There was little to discuss at breakfast. Dante did not have anyone with him in the hideout that knew his involvement in what had happened, at least not the extent to which he and the state of California were involved. The security personnel were not in Dante's inner circle as far as policy and conspiracy were involved. He relied on them to protect him, but had little use for them beyond that. He felt distinctly alone at the breakfast table, barely able to enjoy the French toast and avocado he was dining on. Bringing his chef along had been a good idea. The food was good even if he was having trouble appreciating it right now.

The news media were relentless in reporting on the possible involvement of California in the attacks on Texas. They barely discussed the assassination of Maxwell at all. Either they had not made the connection or they felt it was not important enough to matter. Perhaps they even felt it was justified to some degree. The war on the media that the current President had waged had taken a certain toll on the progressive control it once enjoyed. Conservative media sources had been on the rise for a few years, to a point now where there was almost a balance in reporting. Dante watched with horror as investigative reporters from every channel tied him to the attacks, to the professor, to Capo. An expert in body language was analyzing his most recent press conference, concluding Dante was a terrorist.

At this point, the sanctions Governor Leland had ordered seemed a grossly disproportionate response, even to Dante. They would be damaging to California's struggling economy, particularly the energy embargo, but he was willing to accept them indefinitely if that was the totality of the retaliation by Texas. He felt sure that it was not.

"Governor, Julie has been buried out by the garden," said the chief of security. A large man with dark hair and a goatee, he had taken it upon himself to dispose of her body without any official investigation, given the current need for discretion.

"Thank you, Darrell," Dante said without looking up. He was disappointed about losing Julie, but not particularly surprised. She would not have handled any of this well. Dante returned his attention to the television coverage. The video of Capo and Adam was being played every hour, and it made him sick.

The confessions of each of the captives directly implicated Dante in the attacks. His denial in response the President's offer for a summit had been completely unconvincing. The only consolation Dante had right now was that very few people knew where he was currently located, and almost of those people who did were here with him. He ran his fingers through his thick black hair. How would he come out the other side of this? Was there the possibility that Texas would impose the sanctions and then let this go at some point? It seemed unlikely, but there were very few alternatives to waiting and seeing. He realized now the mistake of letting Capo run the entire operation with so little oversight. There was supposed to be no connection to California, or to himself. The entire thing was supposed to look like an organic uprising of the Left rising against the conservative state of Texas, a populace sick and tired of conservative governing and no longer simply resisting, but revolting. Once Texas fell, America would change almost all at once. Instead, it was being portrayed as the work of a lunatic governor from a leftwing state. This was exactly the scenario he had hoped to avoid.

Ordering a follow-up attack on Texas was not even an option. Even if he wanted to, there was no one else in line to take that order, Capo had been the only contact for this operation that Dante ever used. Capo being captured was never even the slightest consideration, Dante had never thought that would be possible. Even if there were a broader network to use, Dante was not sure he would order it. The retaliatory strike from Texas was likely be bad enough, but drawing in the federal government would be catastrophic and was sure to happen if he did. This President was no fan of Dante's, or of California in general. Where Texas was sure to be given plenty of leeway in how it responded, California was equally likely to be attacked if it furthered the initiative in any way.

For politicians caught up in scandals it was usually possible to weather the storm if the politician was willing to hang on, at least for progressive politicians. A compliant media would move on quickly to the next scandal or issue and last week's career-ending story was no longer on anyone's mind. Dante was looking at the coverage on the news now and realizing that this was not a strategy he was going to be able to use. He couldn't count on the mainstream media to cover for him anymore, and conservative talk radio and news outlets remained relentless in their coverage, some claiming this was the start of a second Civil War. Waiting this out as a political bump in the road was not realistic in the current environment.

Dante considered the reality that he might need to leave the country. He pondered his options and envisioned very few that included his remaining the governor of California and not spending the rest of his life in prison. He had distant relatives in Italy that would be willing to take him in, at least he hoped they would. Hiding out for the rest of his life on some Italian countryside farm was preferable to sitting in a prison cell, but only marginally so in his mind. He looked at his passport and contemplated how to make the trip undetected. It was a gamble either way. If he waited and the blowback from the attacks did not diminish he would have no opportunity to flee as pressure mounted against him. If he fled now, the case would be made to indict him and the media would portray him as an international fugitive. Italy would cave immediately to the slightest pressure to find him and send him back. Fleeing to a place where no one knew him might be the better option. Dante opened his laptop and began a search for non-extradition countries.

66.

Ray was just getting dressed after shaving and showering when he heard a knock at his door. His heart sped up just a little thinking it was Grace again. He opened the door and saw Clark in the hallway, smiling.

"Morning, Ray," he said. "Grab your jacket and come with me to the Governor's office if you would."

Ray looked at him a little puzzled, it was forty-five minutes before their scheduled morning meeting was to begin and now he felt like he was late for something. "Sorry, Clark, I though the meeting wasn't for a little while," he said while pulling on his sport coat and walking out into the hallway.

"Different meeting, Ray," he said with a curious smile still on his face. "This one's a surprise."

Ray liked Clark more and more as he got to know him. He found him to be very approachable, sincere, and intelligent. Though most of Ray's time was spent working with Grace, his limited interactions with Clark were always positive.

"Ray, what you are going to be offered here by the Governor has been discussed by all of us," Clark said as they walked toward the office. "Grace, Tim, Jack, and I all agree that this should be yours if you want it. I am going to let the Governor ask, but I wanted you to know we all support this, if you are willing."

Ray's heart was racing in his chest. He could tell by the smile on Clark's face that whatever the surprise was, it was a big deal. Clark walked into the Governor's office and Ray followed him in. Seated around the table were Jack, Grace, and Tim. Grace smiled at him, the look in her eyes was soft.

"Have a seat, Ray," Tim said. Ray sat down across from Grace, next to Jack, and folded his hands on the smooth wooden table in front of him. "Ray, you know that I signed that bill making Austin a district of the state now, right?"

"Yes, sir," Ray nodded.

"Well, we modeled it after the District of Columbia in that legislation, but not quite exactly," Tim said. "The district will have its own police force, but the governing body will be a committee of House and Senate members and myself acting as the executive."

"That sounds like a great plan," Ray said, trying to hide his nervousness. He couldn't tell what exactly this would have to do with him, the dissolution of Austin was not even a part of the policy area he had been working on.

"We would like you to run the police department, Ray," Tim looked him in the eyes, examining his reaction.

Ray exhaled deeply, smiling broadly. "I wasn't sure where this was going," he laughed as everyone around him let out a chuckle. He looked at Grace. Her eyes were warm, she was smiling broadly at him. He realized this was probably her idea.

"I would be honored, Governor," he said, standing to shake Tim's hand.

Tim took Ray's hand in a firm grip and smiled at him, slapping him on the shoulder.

"What should we call you," Tim smiled, "Grand Poohbah, Your Royal Highness?" Tim's cop humor returned to him in an instant, and he couldn't resist the teasing.

"Sir, you can call me whatever you want," Ray laughed, "but the title of chief seems just fine."

"Welcome aboard, Ray," Tim smiled. "I am going to leave you with these fine people and go to my room for a bit, let me know if you need anything. As of right now, you are the Chief of Police for the District of Austin Police Department, HR can get you processed so we can actually pay you."

Tim waved to the team and left. The three remaining all shook Ray's hand and congratulated him. Clark motioned for him to sit at the table with them and pulled out a folder.

"Ray, this is yours to make of it what you will, to shape and mold the agency from the ground up," he said to Ray in a sincere tone. "I have a folder here with sixty-four officers that all recently left Austin police department during this craziness, most of them recently joined the Hill Country Militia that you are familiar with, some have been members for much longer."

Ray looked intrigued, sliding the binder over to his side of the table to flip through the background and photographs of the officers.

"You don't have to take any of them, the agency is yours to build," Clark said, "but they are all vetted. Every one of them would love to come back and return their community to what it once was. There is no pressure to take any of them, this is just an offering to help get you started if you want."

"I'll take them all," Ray said, closing the binder. "I will look through it later to get a feel for who they are and where I can put them, but I trust your judgement, Clark."

Clark smiled at him, and squeezed him on the shoulder.

"Ray, my people will help you for as long as you need," Jack said. "I have dispatchers, records clerks, and evidence custodians I can loan you for a while too. We will keep plenty of troopers in the city until you get up to staff."

"I appreciate that, Jack," Ray smiled, "I will need the help for sure."

Ray looked at Grace. His conversation with her and his confession about how much he missed police work flashed through his mind and she could read it on his face. "You'll be great, Chief," she said smiling.

"Those officers in the binder will be at the Austin Police headquarters at 9 a.m. tomorrow morning, Ray," Clark said. "I'd like to bring you over there and introduce you to them if you don't mind."

"I look forward to it," Ray said. His mind was swimming, excitement being the only thing keeping him from feeling completely overwhelmed.

"I have to make a quick call if you don't mind," he said grabbing his phone and stepping out into the hallway. He dialed Dave's number. Dave picked it up on the first ring.

"Hi, Ray!" he said. "How are things going?"

"Hey Dave, they are going really well," he said. Suddenly realizing he was going to miss the Foundation and the people there tremendously. "Dave, I have been offered a position on the Governor's team that I cannot turn down."

Dave laughed, "Congrats, Ray, I have been waiting for this call. I figured it was only a matter of time."

"Dave, I really have enjoyed working with you and the team over there," Ray said, noticeably relaxed by Dave's reception of the news."

"We have enjoyed having you, Ray," Dave said sincerely. "Don't be a stranger, you are always welcome here....once we get a new building," he chuckled.

"I won't, Dave, be safe," Ray said and hung up the phone before walking back into the office. He sat across from Grace, who winked at him, and he looked out the window, unable to contain his grin.

Tim came back into the office a few minutes later for the planned meeting on the folder Grace had put together, pulling Ray back into the reality of what was still happening around him. The decision to appoint Ray to run the new District of Austin Police Department likely meant that the policy assistance he had been giving was no longer needed, the decision or decisions had been made and were likely to be announced right here. Ray was aware that he was a part of history in this moment, whatever was going to happen was going to be announced right here and now. Ray closed the new binder full of his future police officers and nodded at the Governor as he took a seat back at the table with them. Each member pulled out the binders from Grace. The mood in the room shifted to somber.

"I have spent most of the night considering the options laid out by the team at this table," Tim began. "Let me start by saying that I do not take this lightly, and I know that none of you have either. Your recommendations, the sincerity of the consideration with which they were made, have been more valuable to me than anything I can think of in recent history. We are in uncharted waters here, there is no easy path forward."

Tim paused and looked around the table, all eyes were focused intently on him. "We must retaliate for this attack on Texas," he continued slowly, "of that much I am sure." He paused again. "It is not about revenge, it is about justice and closure. I do not want this to escalate further than it already has, but we *will* throw the last punch here. We will ensure that this never happens again, that no one would ever consider attacking our people, our way of life, ever again."

Ray glanced at the team around him. Grace was nodding slightly, though her expression was unchanged. Clark was intently looking at Tim and reading his face, as was Jack.

"My decision at this juncture is to continue the trade sanctions with California and issue a warrant for capital murder for the Governor of California, Dante Malone," Tim paused and exhaled loudly." Ray saw Grace's eyes narrow slightly, he thought for a moment even disapprovingly. "Once the warrant is publicly announced, we will hit his hideout with an airstrike," he said almost painfully.

Grace's eyes returned to normal, a relieved look on her face. Jack and Clark nodded agreement.

"If we take him out in that airstrike, so be it," Tim continued. "If not, we will hunt him down and bring him to justice in Texas, or kill him where we find him. My hope is that we will be able to point to Malone as the most important figure in this attack, leaving Californians as a group blameless and thereby avoiding an all-out war between our two states," Tim paused again. "I realize, as do all of you, that this attack was more about an ideology than it was about two states, and that this will not change that at all, but maybe it will shift the conversation and prevent a breakdown of the Republic." Tim stretched both hands out on the table and looked down at the smooth dark wood for a moment. "We are in a fragile position right now. If we attack California as a state, we will be at war and draw others into it, even this President will have no choice but to become involved. If we focus on Malone, we might bring attention to the "Resistance" movement and stamp it out of existence as a country and not by secession into Red and Blue individual nation states. I feel that doing it this way offers the greatest promise of preserving our nation, and avoiding an escalation into civil war."

Clark spoke first, "Tim, this is well considered, you know that you have all of our backing here. I should point out that as supportive as I am of our President, he should be making statements or providing some leadership here. I am proud of you for filling that void."

"Thank you, Clark," Tim said. "I truly hope we are doing right by the United States with this plan, but regardless, we *will* do right by Texas. We are Texans after all, and at the end of the day we do what we can for the country but we will preserve our state no matter what."

"I will have the warrant for capital murder before noon, Tim," Grace said.

"Good," Tim nodded, "I will hold a press conference at noon tomorrow then. Tim paused for a moment. "I spoke with the adjutant general this morning, the 149th Fighter Wing will be crossing over Arizona during my speech and will hit the hideout shortly after it ends. The entire Texas military will be on high-ready once this commences. I do not anticipate a response by the federal government, but we have to be ready for that as well. California will take time to respond, we will see that coming if they do, but we have a lot of military bases under federal control here that can ramp up in an instant. We will be monitoring their response, but I am hopeful it will not happen without some sort of discussion with the President first, that seems to be more in line with his personality and leadership style. He will be hesitant to get involved, so a rapid retaliation by the feds is highly unlikely." Tim looked at the faces around him, "Would you mind if we prayed for a moment together?"

The group joined hands and bowed their heads. Ray regretted not sitting next to Grace, but pushed it out of his mind. Tim led the group in the Lord's Prayer, after which they all rose to leave.

"Let's all be back here after the press conference tomorrow," Tim said. "Don't stray too far in the time being. I'd like everyone to spend the night here in the mansion again if there are no objections."

There were none.

67.

Manuel Bonilla was thickly muscled, but relatively short. He had been a patrol officer with the California Highway patrol before being assigned to the Governor's protective detail. His accent was thick even though he was born in Miami. Manuel was the son of Cuban refugees and grew up mostly speaking Spanish in his home and his predominantly Cuban community. He walked into the Governor's dining room where Dante was eating a sandwich. Manuel held almost no political ideology, but he held little regard for the Governor, viewing him as weak and cowardly.

"Good afternoon, Governor, you summoned me?" he said.

"Ah, yes, please have a seat Manny," Dante said, looking up from the laptop next to his plate on the table. "Are you hungry?"

"No, sir, but thank you," Manuel replied politely.

"Manny, this conversation is between you and I, it is not for the rest of the team to hear," Dante said, just above a whisper. He continued after Manuel nodded agreement. "You have family in Cuba still?"

"Yes, sir, several aunts and uncles and many cousins," Manuel replied.

"Would you and I be able to take a trip there, stay with someone for a little while maybe?" Dante smiled at him as he spoke.

"Of course, sir, but may I ask the occasion?" Manuel looked puzzled.

"We, you and I, will go there and let some of this news blow over," Dante motioned his hand dismissively, as though it was of minor concern.

Manuel was skilled at reading body language and detecting when a person is lying. In this particular situation, the lie was really not of any concern to him. If the Governor wanted to go to Cuba and stay with his family there, he didn't need to know why. Manuel's family would be honored to have such a guest.

"When shall we leave, sir?" Manuel smiled at Dante.

"Get your things ready, we will need to leave by car at a moment's notice, but I do not know when that moment will come," Dante said. "Just be ready to go at once."

"I am not even unpacked, sir" Manuel responded. "We could leave now if you want."

"Actually, I need you to have one of the other members of the security team take you to get a rental car," Dante told him as he handed him his credit card. "Something low-key, small. I don't want to be noticed in one of those big Suburbans."

"Yes, sir," Manuel said as he moved to the door. "Sir, we cannot *drive* Cuba."

"Yes, I know, Manny," Dante said dismissively. "We will charter a boat after we drive to Florida."

Manuel summoned another member of the security team to pick him up at the house and began dialing to arrange a rental vehicle for pick up.

68

With things returning to normal at the capitol, the cafe and grill inside was finally reopened. The security presence throughout the building was heavy, but there was sense of returning normalcy. Ray sat at a table with Grace eating lunch. He enjoyed her company more than anyone he could remember, but he was still a little nervous around her. The topic of her surprise kiss last night did not come up, but she did not show any indication of being self-conscious about it either. Grace did not ever appear uncomfortable around anyone, she always projected poise and confidence. Ray thought to himself that she would have made a great cop.

"I don't know how to thank you," Ray said looking at her sincerely.

"For what?" Grace said with a smirk on her face as she poked at her salad.

"Right," Ray laughed, "it's just a coincidence that I was whining to you about missing police work and then I get appointed as chief of the new police department here."

"Heck of a coincidence," Grace laughed. "Seriously though, you were the first on everyone's mind when it came up. I might have just been a little more persistent in keeping your name the *only* one on everyone's mind."

"Well then, thank you for that," Ray said smiling at her. He admired how she could look so different but yet so fantastic in any setting. Business suit to sweatshirt, hair up or down, glasses on or off, there was no look that didn't fit her perfectly.

"Are you excited?" Grace asked, smiling.

"More than you know," Ray replied, lifting a slice of smoked brisket with his fork. "But, between you and I, I am a little nervous."

"About what?" she asked.

"Well," Ray said, "it's been awhile since I was a cop, and the department I was on was a smaller suburb. This is a big undertaking, a big department, and some of the guys in that folder Clark gave me have way more experience than I do. I am not sure how they will take to me."

"Clark said he vetted those people," she said in a more serious tone, "vetted them for personality and comportment. Clark is good at reading people, he would know how this mix would go. He wouldn't give you someone who would be a problem."

"Oh, I trust Clark completely," Ray reassured her, "I think I just have a little stage fright is all."

Grace smiled at him and then changed the subject to Ray's children. Ray shifted in his chair just enough that she detected he was uncomfortable.

"I'm sorry, if you don't want to talk about it," she said shaking her head.

"No, no, I love talking about my kids," he interrupted her. "It's just that, well, I was a pretty crappy father, still am I guess. I only see them occasionally. We get along fine, but it is an awkward relationship. I love them more than anything, but for the most part I just provide for them. Marie does all of the parenting. Heck, my daughter calls me Ray more often than she calls me Dad if that gives you any idea of how it is."

"Daughters and their fathers are a special thing," she said soothingly. "She'll remember that you provided for the family, it will give her comfort even if everything else was strained."

Ray looked at Grace's bright green eyes, sparkling even in the florescent lighting of the café. "Thank you for that."

"Are you able to see them whenever you want or, do you have visitation?" she asked.

"Marie is pretty good about letting me see them, except when she gets mad at me," he smiled, "which is most of the time."

"What do you do to make her mad at you?" Grace chuckled.

"Breathe, apparently," Ray smiled.

When they finished lunch, Ray took a walk around the capitol building. He called Marie but she did not answer so he left her a message.

"Marie, it's Ray, I just wanted to tell you that I have been appointed as the Chief of Police for Austin and I will be switching health insurance and all of that stuff, so I will keep you posted on it. Hope all is well with you and the kids."

When he hung up, he thought about how strange it was to give her so little information. Years ago he would have been giving her the play-by play on his career, now he left a thirty second message to tell her some of the biggest news in his life. Half of that was to reassure her that the kids still would have health insurance. Times had certainly changed. He felt a little guilty about not letting her know what was about to happen, but he did not anticipate any immediate cause for concern with the planned attack. As Tim had pointed out, the biggest potential threats were from California or the feds, neither of which was likely to take immediate action.

69.

Special Agent in Charge Leon McAvoy hung up the phone and looked at the agents sitting across from him at his desk in the Los Angeles field office of the FBI. They looked intently at him with emotionless eyes. Agents Tarsa and Devin were veteran agents assigned to the counter-terror division and were unsure why they had been called to McAvoy's office. McAvoy tapped his fingers on the desk for a second, then began. "That was the Attorney General," he said to them in a serious tone. "The President wants Dante Malone, the Governor of California, charged with terrorism."

The two agents looked at each other and then back at him.

"Seems he is worried that this could turn into some sort of civil war," Leon explained. "He believes that charging and arresting Malone as an individual engaged in terrorism relieves the state-to-state tension between Texas and California. He is also no fan of Malone's. The AG wants us to find Malone and arrest him, make it a public event, bring media with you. He has a US attorney getting an arrest warrant for Malone as we speak. No one has seen him since the last press conference, so we assume he is in hiding. Time is of the essence here, he wants him in custody yesterday. Find him, and arrest him. Now."

Tarsa and Devin went to the locker room and retrieved their body armor and MP-10's from their lockers. They headed toward the holding room to speak to a certain professor of biology that they had found handcuffed to their railing a week ago.

As they walked past his office, Leon yelled out to them, "I have ten US Marshalls on their way here to assist you." The agents simply nodded and continued on their mission to extract information on the whereabouts of Dante Malone's hideout.

"Where is Malone's bunker?" Tarsa asked looking at Stevens, who was handcuffed to a bench in the holding room.

"I told those guys the GPS coordinates already," Stevens said fearfully. The seriousness of the agents intimidated him, and he longed for a safe space like they had on his campus.

"We have told you before," Tarsa said, visibly annoyed, "those guys are not with us. We only have what they played on the video they gave to the media, which obviously was not everything."

Don Stevens quickly recited the GPS coordinates of the hideout that Capo had told him to memorize. The agents left the room as quickly as they had entered.

"When am I getting out?" Stevens yelled to them as the door closed.

"We'll be back in a minute," Tarsa yelled from the hallway.

70.

Ray sat on the bed in the Governor's mansion, flipping through the files on the officers that he would meet in the morning. They were an impressive group, each had between ten and twenty-five years on the job. There were two former commanders, a couple of captains, ten sergeants, and the remaining were patrol officers. He was excited to meet them, but still mildly anxious about how he would be received by them. He was an outsider here, and in comparison to a few of them, less qualified for the position.

He reassured himself that these were cops, people he would always be able to get along with. Clark was a good judge of character and Ray knew he would be especially picky in selecting people for this task. Ray trusted him, everything would be ok. He breathed in deeply, realizing he felt more alive now than he had any day since the day he retired. He pondered what he would say to these men tomorrow morning.

He took a sip of bourbon and his mind drifted to the room next to his. He wondered what Grace was doing right now. Nothing about their kiss had been brought up today, and yet there was no awkwardness between them at all. He resigned himself to the fact that he was falling for her. It would not be such a big deal, it's not like he didn't find women attractive despite his resolution to avoid relationships, but this time was different for a couple of reasons. First, he didn't just find Grace attractive, he found her irresistible. Second, she was showing interest in return, something he had not allowed for many years simply by avoiding situations where it could occur. Ray took another sip of bourbon, then laid the folder on the nightstand and put his glass on a slate coaster.

He stood up and started toward the door, stopped midway, then went back and sat on the bed with his head resting in his hands. So much was happening right now. He was starting a new job *and* Texas would attempt to take out the Governor of California tomorrow. Did he really need to add any more to the mix? He stood up again and walked to the door, hesitated, then opened it.

The hallway seemed longer than he remembered as he approached Grace's room. He stopped in front of her door and stared down at the floor for a minute. He was frozen, unsure if he should knock or turn back around. He wasn't even sure what he was going to her for, but he knew for sure that he wanted to see her. As he raised his hand to knock on the door, it opened. Grace took his hand and brought him into her room. Her perfume was faint, but sweet and floral. Barefoot in just a long t-shirt, her legs were athletic and toned. She reached both hands to Ray's face, gently, then brought her mouth to his and kissed him deeply. Ray reached behind her back, pulling her to him closely. Parting lips, they looked at each other momentarily. Ray saw a longing in Grace's eyes, and this time he moved his mouth to hers, kissing her longer, deeper than the last.

71.

Ray woke up to the alarm next to his nightstand, having returned to his room a few hours ago. The last thing he wanted was for Clark or anyone else to see him leaving Grace's room in the morning. He quickly shaved and showered before putting on a shirt and tie. He had just finished tying his shoes when he heard a knock at the door.

Damn it, Clark, I still have twenty minutes, he thought to himself as he went to the door. When he opened it, Grace was there smiling.

"Just wanted to wish you good luck this morning," she said.

"Thank you," he smiled back at her.

"Clark says he will meet you down in the Suburban when you are ready," she said. "Jack is going to drive both of you to the headquarters, and he has a small security team with him."

"Ok, great," Ray said. "Grace, I, just wanted to say," he hesitated looking at the floor.

"Me too," she smiled at him and then turned to walk toward the Governor's office. He watched her walk away, smiling to himself as she went.

When Ray got down to the black Suburban parked in front of the mansion, Clark and Jack were already inside. Clark was in the back seat with the security team and motioned for Ray to get in the front passenger seat. Ray jumped in and Jack headed toward the Police Department headquarters just a few blocks away. The members of the DPS SWAT team that accompanied them congratulated Ray on his new position. It warmed him to be in a vehicle full of cops again.

"You will like this group of officers, Ray," Clark said from behind him. "Top quality professionals. Loyal, and highly skilled."

"Sounds like a perfect team," Ray said. "Maybe I won't even hire any more, we'll cover all of Austin with just these 60 officers," he chuckled.

Clark laughed, "That might be a stretch, even for these guys."

The Suburban pulled in front of the police station. Ray noticed the front window on the right side of the door was boarded up in plywood. As they walked into the building, there were papers and garbage strewn about. Ray was initially surprised, he hadn't considered the possibility that the police station would be vandalized but then realized that most of this damage was probably done by the last group of officers before they left after the former chief had been killed. It was the final anti-cop action they would get to take while still wearing the badges they despised.

As they moved into the training auditorium, Ray could hear a measured hum of conversation. He thought to himself that this must truly be a mature group of professionals. He would have expected a raucous scene with this many cops sitting in a room waiting on someone to come in to talk to them. As he walked in behind Clark and Jack, the group rose to their feet. Moving to the front of the room he scanned their faces. Where had expected a certain amount of scrutiny, perhaps skepticism, he saw none. To a man, their faces were welcoming, expectant.

Clark walked up to the front of the room, standing at a podium. Jack and Ray sat in chairs next to him and the group of officers took their seats as well. The room was silent for a moment, then Clark began.

"Gentlemen, thank you for agreeing to be part of the rebuilding of your community," he looked at them with sincerity. "We are no strangers to one another, but I would like to introduce you to your new chief. Ray Tucker comes to us as a retired police officer from Illinois, you'll figure that out as soon as he starts talking," he smiled and the crowd chuckled. "He has experience in training, SWAT, supervision, patrol, investigations, you name it."

Ray felt uncomfortable, he never inflated his credentials intentionally so he was hopeful Clark would not do it either. So far, this was an accurate assessment of his career. Ray held a particular aversion to people who pretended to have done more than they really have.

"Most recently he has been a policy analyst for our friends at the Liberty Policy Foundation and has been on loan to myself and AG Headey for a couple of weeks now in the aftermath of the attacks," Clark continued. "He has been chosen by the Governor to lead this new agency, the District of Austin Police Department, has selected all of you here today to be founding members of his new agency. Let's give him a warm welcome."

The crowd took to their feet and applauded Ray as he approached the podium and shook hands with Clark. A few hoots and hollers reassured him that he was among a group of cops. Nervous though he was, Ray could not remove the smile from his face as he looked out at the group of men in the audience.

"I would like to begin with a quick story about who I am," Ray began. "I think when I tell it to you, you will know all you need to know about me," he paused and looked down at the podium for a moment, becoming serious. "About five years ago, my wife put down an ultimatum, she was moving to Texas with or without me. Forty Chicago winters had been enough for her and I was eligible to retire so I could decide, move with my family or stay at my job," Ray paused for a second, looking down at the podium. "Twenty years I had been a cop, my entire adult life. The people there, the men and women, had been as much a family to me as anyone else, but a wife and kids are family in a different way."

"I had already chosen my job over my family once before, and against my better judgement I retired early and we moved down here to Texas," he continued. "Now don't get me wrong, I love Texas, and I would have come here eventually, that was always the plan. But I wasn't ready to leave my job. I loved being a cop. I resented my wife for pushing me to this decision, and understandably the marriage did not last long once we got down here," he paused a second time to collect his emotions. The crowd looked at him intently, some nodding.

"All of that is just a little background about how I got here," he continued, "but the story I want you to hear is about my last day at the police department. I was about to address my shift for my last roll call as their commander, and I had decided to read Roosevelt's "The Man in the Arena" quote to them, when it really hit me. I did not expect to have to try to hold back tears, but saying those words while looking at the faces of my brothers and sisters sitting in front of me, well," Ray paused for a second as that compartment in his mind broke open and flooded his thoughts. "Anyway, I made it through that short speech, barely, and went back to my office to finish packing my things."

"Throughout the shift, as I packed up the few things I had left in my office, my patrol officers came in to wish me tearful goodbyes," Ray continued. "I barely held it together after each of them left. When the shift ended and I walked out to my car, the shift sergeant, who would be taking my place as commander the next day, had the whole shift lined up in their squads and they escorted me to the edge of town with lights and sirens," Ray paused because he could feel tears welling up in his eyes, he tried to push the emotion back into its compartment again. A few of the members of the crowd rubbed at their own eyes.

"As I drove in the middle of the pack of squad cars, it struck me that I would never do this again," he continued. "I would never again be in a pack of squad cars, surrounded by brave men and women that I would kill or die for, going to a call that the rest of society would run from. As their lights faded in my rear view mirror once I left town, I had to pull over. I called my wife to tell her I was on my way home and I could barely speak," Ray said, more confident now. "I realized that I was doing this for my wife, but I was leaving behind people who were every bit a family to me as she was, and I didn't even want to talk to her at that point."

"I tell you this not to make you sad or because I want some sort of pity, but quite the opposite," Ray continued. "I want you to know how much policing means to me, and what it means to me. I also tell you this because I am fully aware that this scenario was denied for all of you here today," more heads nodded in the crowd, a few more officers rubbed their eyes. "As sad as that day was, I was at least able to cherish my final day with my brothers and sisters in celebration. I was blessed. I know that most of you were forced to leave in an instant and worked in an agency you had grown to despise," Ray said to a visibly emotional crowd. "That last day, the memory of your brothers and sisters celebrating your career, was stolen from you."

"Well, we are back, all of us," he smiled, his voice gaining volume. "We are a new family, one that will be able to cherish every day that we can do this job and we will be here for one another, always." The group of officers rose to their feet, applauding and whistling. As they settled back down and took their seats, Ray continued in a more business-like manner.

"Thank you, sincerely, for that and for being here," he said. "I have to head back for a meeting with the Governor now, but I will be here tomorrow morning to formally meet all of you and we can begin discussing the organizational chart and all of that good stuff. Let's meet back here at 10 a.m. tomorrow," he said. "All of you are getting paid as of today, so feel free to do a little clean-up if you are so compelled, this is our station, make of it what you will."

The group jumped to their feet and began grabbing brooms and garbage cans. Ray smiled at their zeal, he already liked them all. He turned to Clark and Jack who were clapping and reached out to shake his hand. The three of them then headed for the Suburban full of security agents waiting to take them to mansion to await the Governor's announcement in a couple of hours.

"That went really well, Ray," Clark said as they drove toward the mansion.

"I agree," Jack said, "you had me tearing up behind you."

"Thank you both," Ray said, "It was therapeutic for me to say it, I have never told that whole story to anyone."

"If anyone in that crowd had any hesitations about you running the ship, they don't anymore," Clark smiled at him.

"What's plan for today?" Ray asked.

"Mostly sit and wait and see what happens, just provide support for Tim," Clark said. "He wants to do a quick briefing with our team before he addresses the cameras."

"On a different but related note," Jack said, "our team in New York is finding some very interesting information."

"Yes," Clark said, "it is a bit disturbing."

"How so?" Ray asked.

"That other plot was bigger than just the professor at UCLA apparently," Clark said, not getting into specifics in front of the security agents. Jack nodded in agreement. "We'll get into it more after the press conference ends."

Ray sat back in the seat and pondered the consequences of this new information. Adding New York into this mix would likely make a war unavoidable if this could no longer be simply assigned to a group of crazies in California, or just the Dante anymore. He also considered that it was still possible to avoid a war between the states if it were deemed a nationwide terrorist plot rather than tied to the states, assuming there were no further government officials in New York or California discovered as participants. Ray would have to think about how that might play out, and how it could be messaged as a terrorist group rather than the alternative. Ray was going to have his hands full running a new police department tomorrow, so he was not sure how much time he could invest in these policy issues anymore. At least they were in good hands with Clark and Grace, their instincts were the same as his and they seemed a step ahead of him all the time anyway.

Ray realized that he had not thought about Marie and the kids very much with everything else that was going on, despite telling his new officers how she had been the reason for leaving his beloved career. He suddenly felt a little guilty discussing that with a group of people he hardly knew, but quickly brushed it off. He was content that she and the kids lived in an area that was far from what he would consider high risk. Their home was far enough out in the country that things would have to get truly bad before they would be affected. Stephenville was far enough away that even another attack on that area seemed, as highly unlikely as it would be, would not affect them directly. It had simply been poor timing that they were there when the last attack happened. Regardless, Marie had not responded to his voicemail message from yesterday, so he sent her a text message: *stay in today, monitor the news. Governor is speaking at noon.*

72.

Professor Don Stevens was quick to reveal Dante Malone's hidden home in Lake Tahoe. He had memorized the address, he explained to Agent Tarsa, at the encouragement of Capo, who had given him the information.

"He told me to memorize it, just in case I ever needed it," Don nervously mumbled. He was having chronic panic attacks while in custody, and appeared to be on the verge of a complete breakdown.

Tarsa had taken a video of the interview on his cellphone, and jotted down the coordinated on a notepad. "Lock him back up," Tarsa told the attendant in the holding cell area, insensitive to the professor's condition. Tarsa despised Don Stevens, he considered him no better than any other terrorist he had spent his career hunting.

Three black Ford Expeditions awaiting the team in front of the building, along with two local news station vans. The camera crew filmed the Marshalls and the two FBI agents as they got into their vehicles under an agreement that all footage must be held until tonight, after the arrest was made. These two stations would have sole coverage of the arrest, although they had not yet been told who was to be arrested, they were assured that this would be a big story.

When the news cameras had gotten their footage, they asked for a brief interview with Tarsa and Devin.

"Hold the guns up, if you would," the reporter told them as the cameraman zoomed in on their faces. Tarsa and Devin looked at each other and rolled their eyes.

"Could you tell us why you became FBI agents?" the reporter asked with feigned interest.

"I could," Tarsa said curtly, "but I would prefer to get going and you can actually *see* why instead."

The reporter looked scorned, but dutifully packed up her things and got into the van so the group could go to wherever it was they were going. Once everyone was loaded in, the vehicles all began the journey north to arrest the Governor of California on terrorism charges, a destination and mission known only to the federal agents in the lead vehicles.

73

Ray and Grace walked to the café to grab a cup of coffee before meeting with the Governor.

"He's nervous," she said to Ray.

"I don't blame him," Ray said. "We still don't know exactly how this will play out."

"I know," Grace nodded, taking a sip of her coffee. "How did your introduction go?"

"It went really well," Ray smiled. "Great group of guys, we will do good things together."

Grace giggled for a second and Ray looked at her inquisitively.

"Oh, nothing," she smiled, "it's just that I don't notice your Chicago accent that much anymore but sometimes it comes crashing through. Like when you just said that now… 'we will do good things together,'" Grace did her best impersonation of a Chicago accent. She sounded like a female Al Capone.

"Are you making fun of me?" Ray smiled, her impersonation making him chuckle. "This coming from someone who thinks that y'all is a real word."

"It is in Texas," she smiled, her emerald eyes sparkling. Despite everything going on, Grace seemed genuinely happy. Ray hoped at least a part of that happiness was their growing relationship. He wanted to reach out and touch her hand, but that would be completely inappropriate. Anyone watching from the outside might notice the somewhat flirtatious nature of their conversation, but flirting and touching were two very different things. He realized that this relationship would most likely have to remain a secret, perhaps always a secret. He didn't mind, he preferred not sharing her with anyone anyway.

"Let's head back and see if Tim needs anything," Grace said, rising from the table.

When they arrived in Tim's office, Clark and Jack were seated at the conference table but Tim was not there.

"He's coordinating with the military in the other room," Clark said. "He wants the strike to happen right after his press conference ends so they are working out the timing."

"Ok, how's he doing?" Grace asked.

"He's doing fine, just a little nervous," Clark said. "All of this falls on him, you know. No one cares that we advised him, or that the Legislature supports him. At the end of the day, he called the shot, literally, and it is all on his shoulders. I don't envy his position right now."

Grace nodded. Ray turned to Jack and asked, "Any intelligence on Resistance groups that might consider retaliation?"

"No, none," Jack said. "They have been, how should I put it, mostly purged from Austin and never really had a heavy presence anywhere else in the state."

"Purged?" Ray asked.

"Local militias or just vigilante groups have killed a lot of people here in that last couple of weeks, Ray," Jack said. "Those that stayed were purged, most fled pretty quickly after that first day or so."

"I didn't realize that, being up in Waco most of that time," Ray said.

"Yeah, we didn't publicize it much. Media types weren't very welcome here either during that time, so it did not get much coverage."

"How many dead?" Ray asked.

"No idea," Jack said, looking at him solemnly. "From what we can tell, the groups were pretty selective in their killings, limiting it to active Resistance types and anarchists. Not all liberals and progressives, just the radicals. Still, there were a lot of them."

Tim came into the office and sat down with the group, placing his cup of coffee on the table and leaning back in his chair. "Everything is in place," he said. Now it is just waiting."

Grace looked at Tim and said, "Sir, we are all very supportive of your decision here, and we are proud of what you are about to do."

He looked at her and smiled, "thank you Grace. Thank you to all of you."

74

The news caught Dante's attention. The Governor of Texas was going to hold a press conference at noon, central time. He looked at his watch, having ditched his cellular phone on his way up to the hideout. He had roughly a half hour before he would hear what that maniac from Texas was planning to do. He assumed that would be what the press conference was about, what else could it be about?

He stood and went to the window. Manuel was pulling up into the driveway in a rented Chrysler minivan. The two K-9's out front barked at the vehicle they didn't recognize, but settled down once Manuel got out and walked to the front door.

"Start getting your things," Dante barked at him as soon as he walked in. "What took you so long?"

"Sorry, sir, it was a bit of a drive," Manuel answered, heading to his room to get his bag.

Dante went to his room and started packing his bags. Despite telling Manuel to be ready to go, he had done little to get ready himself. After Manuel had loaded his own duffle bag into the minivan, he helped Dante carry his suitcases out to the vehicle, primarily meaning he carried the bags for Dante after he finished packing them. Manuel thought to himself that only a woman would need this much luggage for a trip.

Dante climbed into the rear seat of the minivan. "Leave your phone here, Manny."

"Sir?" Manuel asked. "How will I reach my family, my team?"

"We will get you a new one when we get out of here," Dante said.

Manuel left his cell phone on the porch and got into the driver's seat. Another agent began to approach the car, curious where they were headed, but Manuel shook his head and waved him off. The agent looked confused, but shrugged his shoulders and walked back toward the security house.

"Turn on the news," Dante said form behind him as he started the minivan and did a final look around at his baggage to see that he had everything.

Manuel turned on the local talk radio and it cut in live to the Governor of Texas at a press conference in Austin.

"Turn it up, Manny," Dante said curtly.

Tim's voice came across on the radio as the minivan pulled out of the wooded driveway and onto the winding road to take them out of the valley. "I am announcing that my Attorney General has obtained an arrest warrant for capital murder for Dante Malone, Governor of California, in connection with the horrific attacks throughout the State of Texas a few weeks ago. We request that the Governor turn himself in to the local authorities immediately, and make himself available for extradition to face these charges here as soon as possible."

Manuel looked in the rearview mirror, Dante's face had lost color.

"Let's move faster, Manuel, I want to be in Nevada as soon as possible," he urged. "We can get you a phone there."

As they moved along the winding road, a caravan of black Ford Expeditions and two news vans passed them going the other direction, toward the hideout. Dante ducked down, but it was impossible to see him from outside anyway with the tinted windows. The light gray minivan Manuel had selected did not attract any attention from the federal agents as he passed them. Once they were gone, Dante spun around to watch the group of vehicles as it disappeared around the last bend. There was no doubt who they were and where they were going.

"Maybe they are coming to protect you from the Texans?" Manuel offered as a comforting alternative to what they both already knew was the truth.

"Manuel," Dante said, his tone more personable, "It is you and me now, I will make sure you are handsomely rewarded for getting me to Cuba safely. You can be my only bodyguard, working directly for me. Forget about the pittance the state was paying you."

"Yes, sir," Manuel said as he looked in the mirror at Dante.

Dante was nervous. Manuel would need to believe it was a better deal to stick with him than to give him up. He was reading Manuel to see if he could get an impression of his thoughts, but he found no hint them one way or another.

"We will live like kings in Cuba," Dante smiled warmly at him.

"Sir, Cuba has an extradition treaty with the United States," Manuel pointed out to him. "Are you sure that is where you want to go?"

"They won't enforce it, haven't for a long time," Dante said. "Besides, the Cuban government would be sympathetic to our cause."

"*Our* cause sir?" Manuel looked surprised. "What exactly is our cause?"

Dante was sure that Manuel was becoming suspicious. He had hoped the offer of financial reward would be enough to keep him loyal, but now he was unsure. "Manny, pull over for a second here, I have to piss."

As the minivan came to a halt and Manuel put the car in part, Dante removed a snub nose revolver from his jacket pocket, put it behind Manuel's ear, and pulled the trigger. He dumped Manuel's body out the door and onto the shoulder of the road. As he walked back to the driver's seat, he saw four F-16 jets flying in a low formation toward the hideout. His eyes opened wide as he saw the missiles propel forward from under their wings before they split into pairs of two and headed back the way they had come. A moment later he heard the enormous explosions, and saw smoke begin to billow up from the forest at the exact location he had just left.

Dante blinked, and then ran to the driver's seat and took off in the minivan. He felt lucky, and let out a nervous laugh. "Missed me!" he yelled up at the sky as he sped along the winding roads, further and further away from the smoking reminder of the carnage he left behind.

75.

The report of a successful strike was relayed to Tim's office. The team let out a collective sigh of relief, but then immediately began to anticipate the aftermath. They were monitoring the news and there was no report of it yet, but it had only been fifteen minutes since the hit. A surveillance drone was sending images that showed complete destruction of the home and several vehicles destroyed on the property as well, but the forest canopy made it difficult to get much detail. The drone operator did comment that there were more cares there than they had anticipated.

"What do you think that means?" Tim asked out loud to the team.

"Could be anything, Tim" Clark said. "We were only estimating the number of cars based on Capo's description of the security detail, it might not have been accurate or the Governor might have brought additional cars up there for another purpose."

"Ok," Tim said, "I just hope it wasn't a bunch of civilians."

"Doubtful," Clark said, "Dante had no wife or children and would have wanted to have as few people know about his hideout as possible would be my guess."

The breaking news burst onto the scene about a half hour later and a reporter breathlessly gripped the microphone while talking. "We have a report that up to twelve federal agents and two news crews have been killed in an explosion or series of explosions in a remote area of Lake Tahoe. Local officials are describing this as the biggest loss of federal agents in modern history. Terrorism is on everyone's lips right now."

Every in the room shifted to face the television screen.

"It is unknown why the agents were there or what caused the explosion at this time, and we have no confirmation of which news crews may have also been at this scene or why," the reporter continued. "Reports are limited right now, the government has not commented yet and we still don't know which agency the agents were from."

The team seated around the table looked at one another, confusion on each of their faces.

Tim's desk phone rang and he turned to pick it up. His secretary sounded concerned, "Governor, I have the Attorney General of the United States for you on line one."

"Attorney General Roberts, this is Governor Leland, sir," Tim said into the speakerphone, cautioning those in the room to remain silent by placing his finger to his lips.

"Governor Leland," Frank Roberts began, "what is going on?"

"Sir?" Tim replied.

"Governor, NORAD cleared four Texas F-16's on a training flight through Arizona and up the California border near Nevada today, right where an explosion killed twelve US Marshals and FBI agents."

"I am sorry for your loss, sir," Tim replied.

"That doesn't answer my question, Governor," Roberts persisted.

"Sir, I have no answer for your question at this time," Tim replied. "We are pretty busy her with our own events as you know."

"Governor, I need to brief the President of the United States in five minutes about what happened," Roberts said growing irritated. "I can give him your version or I can fill in the blanks with what I know and or suspect."

"I do not have a version at this time, sir," Tim said, careful not to deny the action.

The Attorney General hung up the phone without saying goodbye.

Tim looked around the table. "What the hell just happened? Why were there federal agents there?" he asked to no one in particular.

"We probably should have asked him," Grace said, "but I don't know how you could have without getting more into the conversation than we would have wanted."

"Exactly," Tim said. "And why were there news crews there?"

"You think they were going to arrest Malone?" Ray asked. "It's not unlike the feds to bring the news with them on a big arrest."

"Could be," Clark said. "Look no further than Waco for a reminder of their tendency to do that."

"How big of a problem is this?" Tim asked, again to no one in particular.

"Well," Grace said, "if we just killed twelve federal agents and a couple of news crews, it's going to be a pretty big problem. We don't have an allowance for collateral damage here."

Jack's cellphone rang and he stood to answer it, moving from the group. After a brief conversation, he placed the phone on speaker on the table. "I think we need to all hear this."

"Everyone this is Mac," came the voice on the other end. "I just saw the coverage on the news, so what I am about to tell you is particularly important. We just finished a videotaped interrogation with a biochemist here in New York. The Resistance was implicated again."

"That's good news," Tim said. "It gives credence to our preventative strike defense since Malone was involved with them as well."

"Right, sir," Mac continued, "but here's the other part. The Governor-elect for New York is also implicated."

The group around the table sat up in their chairs. Now instead of claiming a single madman and a group of terrorists as the problem, the picture of two states coordinating attacks on another state was becoming harder not to see.

"Implicated how," Ray asked.

"He has personally paid for the research and equipment for a bio-attack on Lubbock, Dallas, and Houston out of his campaign funds," Mac said. "At least that is what our friends here told the camera. Both of these biochemists were in California recently. One of them met with both Professor Stevens and Dante Malone on separate occasions to discuss attacks. The Governor-elect was with him on both meetings, while he was a candidate for governor. He offered the assistance of the New York National Guard once he was elected."

"Where are they now?" Tim asked.

"Sir, we are mobile at this time on our way back home," Mac said without specifying his location. "Do you want us to hold off on uploading the videos?"

"Yes, definitely," Tim said. "Nice work, please bring them back along with the videos and we will determine how to approach this new development."

"Roger that, sir," Mac said and then disconnected.

Tim turned to the team at the table. "There is no getting around this now, we will need to put together a package and brief the President," he said shaking his head.

"We can work on that right away," Grace said. "But sir, please ask the President to come here, I am advising you against travelling out of the state at this time."

Tim looked at her incredulously at first, then nodded slowly as what she was saying began to register. If Tim traveled to Washington DC, he would very likely be arrested.

"I will ask him," Tim nodded, "but I am thinking we will get a video conference at best."

"That would work too," Grace said. "I just don't think you should be making that trip right now. If we can make the case to him that the federal government needs to step in, that we acted in defense of the State of Texas, maybe we will get a pass on whatever happened here as well as some assistance in warding off whatever is brewing in New York."

"I think grace is exactly right," Ray said. "We can make the claim that we acted in defense of Texas by hitting Malone, and that those agents were in no way a target of our attack. That is completely believable and we will probably have a sympathetic ear from this President," he continued. "But, the New York development requires action. If we hit them unilaterally like we just did in California without making our case to the President, we will force him to take action against us to protect the nation."

"I agree with both of them," Clark said. "We have to do something about New York, but selective assassinations on governors is going to be a hard sell to the American public. If the President tells us the feds are staying out of it, then we will have to consider our options. I don't see how he could say that at this point, but we should have a contingency plan just in case. Otherwise, this really is a job for the feds. Let them spin however they want, it won't be our problem anymore once they take over."

"Ok," Tim said nodding in agreement. "Jack and Clark, I want you to coordinate with Mac on getting those videos together. I want all of them, the unedited versions that have all of our intel on them, made onto a single video for the President." Tim turned to Grace. "Grace, you and Ray put together an intel briefing package making the case for the feds to intervene in New York as well as defending our actions in California."

Grace and Ray both nodded agreement. Tim looked at the team and said, "This is it, if the President says he is staying out of this or threatens to hold us responsible for our actions in California then we know we are on our own. That means a likely war with New York. And we'll see what happens in California with Malone gone but it could mean war with them as well. If he decides to intervene, most of our involvement is over, I hope."

76.

Dante maintained the speed limit or just above in the minivan as he cruised through the vast deserts of Nevada. He was not sure where to go at this point, Cuba went out the door as soon as he shot Manuel. If he could make it to New York, maybe Preston Johnson would take him in or hide him somewhere. Preston had just won the election for Governor, and Dante recalled him being very ambitious about the Resistance efforts during his meetings with him as a candidate. Of course at the time, Dante didn't think Preston had a chance in hell at winning. He considered him an immature politician when they met, useful in the cause but probably unelectable. Dante had never been more glad to be wrong than right now. He would find a way to connect with Preston once he got closer to New York.

Dante realized that all of the news coverage on the radio thus far was talking about the deaths of those federal agents. No one was talking about the house being his or his whereabouts. He could use this to his advantage for a while he made his way to New York. The people looking for him probably assumed he was dead. The explosions, even the news had not yet picked up that it was an airstrike, that killed the feds was probably not done by the feds. Dante assumed it might have been Texas, but wasn't positive. Either way, both Texas and the federal government probably assumed he was killed in the strike. He needed to make it to New York before he was a wanted man again.

77.

Ray dialed the cellphone number for Danny Edmonds using the file folder Clark had given him for his new officers. Danny had been a commander for Austin Police Department before the mass resignation that he included himself in. He was the highest ranking officer in the folder.

"This is Danny," his voiced said as he picked up.

"Danny, this is Ray Tucker, how are you?" Ray asked.

"Hi there, Chief, I am good, what can I do for you?" Danny was upbeat and energetic.

"Danny, we have a few things going on that I need to attend to with the Governor for a few days," Ray said. "Would you mind letting the team know I will be gone for a couple of days and maybe get everyone situated with equipment and logistics? We were supposed to have that meeting in the morning, but I won't be able to make it."

"Sure thing, Chief," Danny said. "There is plenty to do, we will take care of it, don't you worry about a thing."

"Thank you, Danny, sorry we are meeting like this," Ray apologized. He already liked Danny.

"Not a problem, sir, glad to help," Danny said before disconnecting.

Ray looked over at Grace across the table from him. "Not really the way I wanted to start out at the department, but looks like it is in good hands," he said smiling at her.

"One day you can explain this to them," she smiled, "I have no doubt they will understand completely."

They both leaned back in their chairs and looked at the pile of files and papers in front of them. It was still sinking in for Ray that they had just killed a dozen federal agents and a couple of news crews. It was an accident, of course, but it had still happened. Added to that was the unknown situation in New York. Ray was sure that there was no imminent threat or Mac would have said there was, so at least that pressure was off the table. But there would still need to be some sort of follow-up there.

"Even if Mac and his team have eliminated the threat of attack from New York," he said looking at Grace, "we still have to do something there, right?"

"Absolutely," Grace said. "At a minimum their Governor-elect conspired to conduct a terrorist attack on Texas cities, we will have to respond in some way."

"Do you think Tim will let the President handle it, if he is so inclined?" Ray asked. "I mean, if the feds arrested the Governor-elect on a terrorism charge, we might be able to just let that part go then, right?"

"Yes," Grace agreed, nodding her head. "And I think that is the direction Tim wants this to go, but that completely depends on how the President responds. The reality is that this could go in several directions and I don't know that any one of them is more likely than the other."

"Good point," Ray said.

"If we go after New York," Grace began "then I think they will respond and we are at war. That is one scenario. The feds could also be prompted to action, and we are in a much bigger war. That's another scenario. California could jump in…and so on. Best case scenario is the feds arrest the Governor-elect, make a bunch of related arrests on The Resistance, and this all goes into the history files."

"What about the federal agents that died in the missile strikes?" Ray asked.

"We could still blame that on Malone, kind of like a felony-murder rule scenario," she said.

Ray nodded in agreement, "I see, kind of like if a police officer shoots an innocent person while trying to shoot the guy robbing the bank…the robber gets charged with that person's death, not the cop."

"Exactly," Grace nodded.

78.

The team met in Tim's office after only a few hours of sleep. An entire package was presented to the Governor that included all of the videos of the interrogations of the suspects, unedited, as well as a detailed report showing Dante Malone's involvement and the response that Texas had taken. It also pointed out that the indictment of Malone by the feds was not publicized, and that Texas had no way of knowing that there would be federal law enforcement at the hideaway before launching its attack. The report did not shy away from highlighting the fact that while simultaneously failing to notify anyone in the Texas government about the federal agencies involvement with Malone's hideaway, there was no shortage of media involved, a detail that would not go unnoticed by this President.

"I think we have made our case on every point, Tim," Grace said. "We have laid out the justification for our attack. We have made the case that killing the agents was accidental, and placed the blame for their deaths with Dante Malone. We have also made the case for action against the Governor-elect of New York and for a large number of Resistance members. Most importantly, we have clearly established that the action in New York needs to be initiated by the feds, and what the likely consequences would be if Texas takes action unilaterally. We also leave no doubt that Texas will act if the fed fails to, that the threat to Texas is imminent."

Tim flipped through the pages of the report. "I do have the best team in this country," he said with a smile. "This is excellent. All of you have done a great job."

"Tim," Clark said looking around the table. "I took it upon myself to have the militia head back to New York, along with some Jack's Anti-terror team, just in case it comes down to having to do this alone. I think another airstrike is out of the question. I can pull them back if you don't agree."

"No," Tim nodded, "that was an excellent decision. Let's hope we don't have to use them, but I want them in place for immediate action if we do have to."

"I feel a lot better today than I did yesterday, despite everything that has happened," Tim said. "I think the President will have no option but to act on the information we are giving him. I told his people I would have this to him by tomorrow, but I am going to send it now. I hope we get the response we want."

Before they left the room, Clark sent a text message to Mac:

The whole flock will be migrating North, waiting for the thaw.

Within the hour, just over half of the members Hill Country Militia were headed toward New York, using various routes and multiple cars. DPS Anti-terror teams were also on their way in covert vehicles. Each car knew its assigned target and could act independently of the others. The remaining militia members moved down to Austin in case there was an attempt to take action against the Governor, but the feds or anyone else. They would provide extra security while remaining undetected.

79.

Dante arrived in the suburbs of Chicago sooner than he had planned. He found a Motel 6 on Mannheim Road in Franklin Park and pulled in. He handed the front desk attendant Manuel's driver's license to rent the room, having taken his wallet while he pushed his body off the road. The attendant didn't bother to look at the picture, and there was a close enough resemblance that it wouldn't have drawn the attention of any but the most observant of people anyway. Handing Dante the key to a second floor room, the attendant pointed out the door and to the left.

Dante parked across the lot from his room so he could look down and see the minivan from his window on the second floor. The room was clean, but dated. There was no minibar, no complimentary robes or coffee; just a bed, a desk, and a television. Dante despised the low-class room he was now sitting in, but thought he would draw less attention here than staying at one of his usual hotels on the North Shore or even a few miles away in Rosemont. Dante adored Chicago, and visited as often as he could, so there was the possibility that someone there would recognize him. There would be no time for play here anyway, he was going to get some sleep and then get back on the road toward New York.

Dante tossed a duffle bag onto the bed and opened it. He counted out ten straps of cash, ten thousand dollars in each strap. That should get him through for the time being. He considered using Manuel's credit cards for some of his miscellaneous expenses, but wasn't sure how much money was available on them and wanted to avoid drawing attention by having a card declined. He would just pay for everything with cash for now.

Dante turned on the television and watched the news for a little while. There was still no discussion of the Lake Tahoe place being his. In fact, he was not even mentioned on the news other than a single commentator questioning why he had not even bothered to make a statement about the deaths of the agents in his state. Dante pulled out the pay-as-you-go phone he had picked up in Iowa and activated it with one of Manuel's credit cards. He then called into the local California CNN affiliate and gave a brief on-air statement condemning the attacks on the federal law enforcement agencies. The affiliate's coverage was rebroadcast on the national station almost immediately.

80.

Ray sat up in bed as he heard Dante Malone's voice talking by telephone to a local correspondent in California being rebroadcasted on CNN's cable news.

"That's right, Marsha" Dante's voice could be heard saying as the correspondent looked intently into the camera, "whoever did this should be brought to justice."

"Where are you now, Governor?" Marsha asked. "You have been absent from public for a while now."

"Oh, I am safe and sound and looking forward to getting back to working for the good people of California, Marsha," Dante avoided answering directly.

"Well, Governor, thank you for calling in and reassuring the people of California that you are ok," the correspondent said.

"No problem, Marsha," Dante said. "Let's just hope we can bring justice to the terrorists who killed those agents as soon as possible."

The screen shifted back to the national news station and the anchor said, "Well, there you have it. The Governor of California has condemned the explosions that killed twelve federal law enforcement agents and two news crews as a terrorist attack. This is the first time that we are hearing it officially confirmed as terrorism."

Someone knocking at his door pulled him away from the television screen and he opened it to find Grace standing there. This time she was not dressed in her casual clothes, she had put on business attire and looked serious.

"I just saw it," Ray said.

"Yes, Tim wants us to meet, now," she replied.

"Let me grab my jacket," Ray said leaving the door open. He had not changed out of his dress slacks yet so he was able to throw on his jacket quickly and be on his way. He followed Grace down the hall and into Tim's office where Clark and Jack were already seated. Grace and Ray sat next to them and waited for Tim to come in.

Tim walked in a moment later with a pot of coffee and poured everyone a cup. He sat at the head of the table and leaned back in the leather chair.

"That bastard," he said shaking his head. He wasn't enraged as he had been when he found out Dante was involved in the attack, he was almost amused. "Not only did he apparently escape, but now he is spinning this as a terrorist attack. He has the lapdog media going along with it. When it finally comes out that it was us, well, he has already cornered the narrative. We are now the terrorists."

"Not necessarily," Ray said, cautiously reading the Governor's mood. When Tim looked at him he felt encouraged to continue. "The report that Grace gave you to forward to the President reads in part like an indictment, it lays out exactly how Dante Malone was involved and why he was charged with murder here in Texas. It lays out the justification for the strike, both in terms of retaliation as well as preemption. If anyone looks like a terrorist in the closer examination of everything, it is Dante Malone."

"Right, but only the people in this room and the President of the United States know anything about that report," Tim countered.

"We will likely have to admit that we made the strike at some time," Grace said. "We knew that our refusal to comment was going to be viewed as an admission anyway, that someday we would have to discuss our part in the strike. This is just a lot sooner than we anticipated. On the bright side, we have the document ready to make our case, as well as the videos made by Mac and his team. When we do release everything, we will win the public opinion back pretty quickly, at least of those that can be won."

"The President could classify that whole report when he looks at it tomorrow," Tim pointed out. "If he does that, no one will ever see it."

"Sir," Clark said, "if he does that then that means he will also be refusing to take any action against the threat in New York. We will be put into a position to decide if we want to act on our own."

"We have already made the decision that we will," Tim said, confirming what Clark was alluding to.

"Well then," Clark continued, "we will mount our own media campaign as well. Releasing classified documents at that point will be the least of our concerns. At least we can still win the public opinion battle with those willing to listen, as Grace pointed out."

"Yes," Ray jumped in, "at that point we would be looking to recruit allies or to at least keep others in neutral grounds. The report will do that to the extent either is possible."

"Ok," Tim said, sounding relatively relaxed, "let's see what the President has to say tomorrow. We have a teleconference with him at noon. We will go from there I suppose." Turning to Jack he added, "Why don't you have your people see if they can get a lead on that phone call, where it came from. Probably a longshot but we could at least try."

"Will do," Jack nodded and got on his cellphone.

"Let's meet back here at 11:45 and prep for the teleconference with the President," Tim said to the team. "Not much to go over, we will mostly be listening I expect."

Ray and Grace walked back to their rooms together, being located in the opposite hallway from where Jack and Clark were staying. When they got to Grace's room, she glanced back down the hallway before looking him in the eyes. "Are you coming in for little bit?" she asked with a slight smile.

"I would love to," Ray smiled back. Grace grabbed his belt buckle and pulled him into her room before closing the door behind them.

81.

Preston Johnson answered the phone even though he did not recognize the number. "Preston, here."

"Preston, this is Dante Malone, how are you my friend," Dante said as friendly as he could pretend to be. He was concerned how he would be received by Preston, given the news in the media of the past few weeks.

"Dante!" Preston nearly screamed, leaving Dante reassured of his support. "My goodness, how are you?"

"Well first, let me say congratulations on winning the gubernatorial election in New York," Dante said. "You are in an elite club now, only fifty members."

"Oh, thank you so much, Dante," Preston replied.

"Preston, I assume you have seen the news," Dante said. "What are your thoughts on me coming to stay with you for a while to let things cool down in California a bit?"

"Dante, it would be my honor to have you stay with me," Preston said. "Given everything that is happening, and with the plans we are working on here in New York, your timing is impeccable," he laughed. "I have a place for you that no one will be able to find. You will be safe, and we can continue the incredible work that you have already started. You are a legend among the Resistance here, my friend. Having you come to stay with me is like having royalty visit."

"You are too kind, my friend," Dante replied, becoming somewhat intoxicated by the compliments. "I am just about to Ohio, Preston, can I call you when I get to New York and we can figure out the details?"

"Yes, do that," Preston said. "I am so happy you are coming here, talk to you soon. Drive safely."

Dante hung up the phone and breathed a sigh of relief. Now he had a place to stay and someone to help him. Not just anyone, either. The Governor-elect of New York. Things were improving by the minute. He arched his back to stretch, the mattress in that motel has left his back aching. *No more of that*, he thought to himself. He would be living in the standard he was accustomed to from now on. He was sure that Preston would accommodate his tastes and he would not have to feel like he was hiding any longer, even if he kind of was.

82

Grace was resting her head on Ray's chest, her foot smoothly sliding along his lower leg. Her finger gently traced the snake on his forearm as he gently stroked her hair.

"I want to wake up to you one day," she whispered, knowing he would need to leave for his room momentarily.

"Me too," Ray said softly. "When this is all over, when we return to something more normal, I hope that we are able to do that."

"More normal than sleeping together in the Governor's mansion just before the outbreak of the second Civil War you mean?" she giggled.

"Yes, more normal than that," he laughed.

"I can tell that you are reluctant to engage in a relationship, Ray," she said, "and I understand why. I am not going to ask anything of you that you can't give, or don't want to give."

"I have never met anyone like you, Grace," Ray whispered. "I have not wanted to be in a relationship since my divorce, I had written that part of my life off as being over. Meeting you has made me think about life a little differently. I feel like you know who I am, what I am. If you are ok with that, I want to give you whatever I can."

Grace looked up at him, her bright green eyes almost glowing in the dim light of the room. She kissed him softly on the lips and whispered "good night" to him as he got up to leave.

"See you in the morning," he whispered to her.

When Ray got back to his room, he briefly flipped through the report again. The information about the Governor-elect in New York jumped out at him for a reason he could not make sense of. He had a strange feeling that the incoming governor might know something about where Dante Malone was hiding. He hadn't considered it before, probably because he had assumed that Dante was dead, but now that the dust was settling he was considering it. He wrote a note to himself on a notepad to discuss the possibility with Jack and Clark in the morning. He took a sip of bourbon from the glass on his nightstand, thought about Grace for a moment, then went to sleep.

83.

The DPS Anti-terror teams had just settled in to watch the Governor-elect. Four separate surveillance teams could view now his residence from various locations, leaving no gaps in the observation timeline. There were eyes on both entrance doors to the modest Pine Hills six flat apartment complex where Preston was staying while waiting to move in to the Governor's Executive Mansion officially. Curtains preventing looking directly into his third floor apartment, but a window in the building's hallway gave one of the teams a view of his door, the only entrance to his unit other than the window. The tech team was able to isolate audio monitoring of the unit with some success, though they would know better once the building came awake and its occupants began communicating with each other and making other kinds of noise. For now, the only intelligence the audio monitor was able to provide was positive confirmation that Preston snores, loudly.

There were another forty men from the Hill Country Militia strategically positioned around the city ready to follow Preston anywhere he went. Four men per vehicle, in ten vehicles, all of them with the singular purpose of capturing or killing Preston as soon as they were ordered to do so. The Hill Country Militia's presence here was undetected, and would remain so as long as possible, but any covert action or contact would fall to them. The plan was to keep the DPS Anti-terror teams away from detection, allowing for official deniability in the event of an incident involving the militia group. The two remained in contact only through the DPS team leader and Mac, both using throw-away phones. Communications between the members of each team was done solely through encrypted radio transmissions, which were kept to an absolute minimum. The apartment was located far enough away from the Albany mansion that the groups were unlikely to be detected by the Governor's security teams, but that could change if Preston went mobile, he was likely to already have some sort of security detail attached to him. None had been detected by any of the DPS teams or the militia teams, but they could be static teams only used for transportation, in which case they might show up right when the teams took action. In any case, they didn't seem to prevent a problem at the time.

The men had sequestered their long guns away in the rear compartments of their vehicles, relying only on their handguns for now. The handguns were less likely to be noticed if any were stopped local law enforcement. The environment and suburban terrain also meant that contact would be close quarters, not like the rolling hills surrounding the Speaker's residence in California. Seth's sniper rifle would not be needed here unless the scenario changed drastically.

Mac looked over at Seth in the back seat while Dave drove and Joe sat in front of him. They were trying to look inconspicuous by maintaining a normal speed and varying their routes, waiting for any information from the DPS surveillance teams to indicate activity.

"I offered to have our teams do some recon on the Lake Tahoe residence, make sure we got him," Mac said referring to the news that Dante was still alive. "I think we all were a little too confident that it was an easy mark, and wasn't worth the risk of getting caught there. In hindsight, we should done the recon and called in the strike from the ground."

"No need to second guess the op now, Mac," Seth said. "Everyone did their part, and I don't blame the Governor for trying to avoid getting us mixed up in anything on the ground at that time. I think the fact that we are here now shows that he is learning as we go along as well."

"Yeah," Joe said with a sarcastic grin on his face, "except this time we don't have the option of air support. We are on our own."

"I like the terrain here if it comes to that," Mac said. "We make it out to the woods here, and there are plenty, and we could disappear like melting snow."

Mac's phone rang and he saw it was Lt. Longi, the DPS team leader calling.

"Joe, it's Mac," he said answering on the first ring.

"Mac, just letting you know that the light came on in his apartment," Joe said. "He's awake and moving around. Sounds like he is typing on a computer right now. We'll keep you posted."

Mac hung up and turned back to his team. "He's up and at 'em early it sounds like. We'll see what the day holds for us."

84.

Ray sat down in the café with Clark, Grace, and Jack to have coffee and relax before the briefing with Tim and the teleconference with the President.

"Last night I thought about something," Ray said to the group, "with Dante making it out of that airstrike alive, however that happened, is there a chance he will try to make it to New York and meet up with the Governor-elect?"

"Hmm," Clark said, tapping on his coffee cup. "That is a possibility. He would realize by now that we found him in his most secret hiding place in California, I could see him making a run for it across the country and hiding out in Albany."

"That presents a unique problem if he does," Ray said. "I assume we would still want to take him out or capture him, right?"

"Absolutely," Grace said as Clark and Jack nodded.

"Well," Ray continued, "we would have a difficult time not bringing New York into the fray if we capture or kill Dante in their state and do the same with their incoming governor. Assuming, of course, that the President doesn't make this a federal issue once we have this conference call."

"Yes," Clark said. "Good point. I am going to ask Tim to move the meeting up an hour so we can have a contingency plan in place should he show up in New York."

"Sounds good," Ray said as he stood up, "I am going to go back to my room and work on some scenarios to give to the Governor then."

Ray headed back to his room in the mansion and began to play out some scenarios n his mind. The easiest plan would be to simply have the militia take out both men when they found them, preferably together. The most difficult would be capturing both and bringing them back to Texas to face trial. The Governor-elect would likely have some security with him, escalating the possibility of a violent confrontation.

Ray drew up three scenarios. The first was the easiest the one Ray hoped would happen. If the President told them during the teleconference that the feds would take over the investigation, then DPS could simply provide the intel to the feds and standby while the feds did their thing. That could mean anything from arresting them to burning down the building, both were possible once the feds were on the scene as history showed.

The second scenario would be that the President defers again to the states to solve their own problems. This would leave the second and third options on the table. One would be to have the Mac's team terminate both men immediately and again deny any involvement. The second would be to capture both men, and have them transported back to Texas by the DPS Anti-terror teams to face charges of murder and conspiracy to commit terrorism. This would be a fully acknowledged official action.

The problem with the last option, as Ray saw it, was that there would likely be resistance during the capture, some of the Governor-elect's security team were likely to be killed. This could lead to an escalation with New York, same as an overt assassination attempt would. Ray came to the conclusion that the only sure way to avoid war was going to be if the President used the fed's jurisdiction to take all of this over. Ray would need to explain to the Governor that he must press that line of thinking with the President if they were to avoid an escalating conflict.

A knock at his door brought him to his feet. He opened the door and saw Grace and Clark there.

"Tim wants us to come in early, do you have some ideas to share with him?" Clark asked as they walked down the hall to the Governor's office.

"I do, should we talk first?" Ray asked.

"No, we can discuss it as a group," Clark replied. "Tim is looking for a consensus on this, so that would be appropriate here. Make the recommendations as you see fit and we can discuss them."

When they entered the office, Jack and Tim were huddled in tense conversation. Tim motioned for them to come and sit down before telling Jack to fill them in.

"The DPS team up in New York just reported that Dante Malone showed up at Preston Johnson's apartment about twenty minutes ago," Jack said. "You called it, Ray."

"This changes things, now, doesn't it?" Tim asked, more of an observation than a question.

"Yes, sir, a little," Ray said. "We discussed this possibility a little during coffee and I drew up a few scenarios."

"Let's hear them," Tim said.

Ray spent the next fifteen minutes going over the scenarios he had put together in his room. The room sat quietly listening to him without interruption. When he had finished, they all paused to consider the possibilities.

"I don't disagree with anything Ray said," Clark volunteered. "Looking around the table, I see that I am not alone. The question then before us is what is our plan going to be?"

"I think we are in all in agreement that the first plan, kicking this to the feds, is most preferable," Tim said as the others nodded agreement.

"Sir, if I may make a recommendation on that front?" Ray said, raising his hand slightly.

"Of course," Tim replied.

"You may want to press that option hard," Ray said. "I think you might need to point out to the President that this will escalate quickly if he does not get the feds involved. Maybe point out to him that we are willing to go to war with New York and California if he doesn't. Perhaps even threaten that we *will* go to war with them if he fails to take action."

"I don't like to bluff," Tim said cautiously.

"I am not sure it would be a bluff, sir," Ray said. "First of all, no one but the President would know you said it so it's not quite like making a bluff to the press. But more importantly, we may be going to war whether we want to or not if either of the contingency plans go badly. I don't think anyone would accuse you of bluffing in this scenario."

"I agree," Grace said. "If you don't spell it out exactly for this President, he very well may defer back to us, which will likely mean war."

"We have a lot of boots on the ground in New York, sir," Clark said. "The longer they are there, the more likely there will be a confrontation. The President will need to give us an answer now, not later. This is probably the best way to push him to one."

Tim leaned back in his chair and ran his hands through his hair. "I agree," he said after thinking for a moment. "Jack, have your men keep track of Dante and Preston at all times." Tim paused for a moment and pointed to Clark. "Have the militia teams ready to take action upon my order, tell them to expect that order shortly after the conference call with the President. When I give the word, they are to capture both men if possible, or kill them if they can't. I want the militia to do that part," he said nodding. "If they do capture them, I want DPS to take them and bring them back here to Texas. We probably don't want to publicize another assassination, but I am ok with everyone knowing we did our own extradition on a couple of terrorists."

The group around the table nodded. Jack and Clark began sending text messages to relay the orders and to put the teams on standby.

"Grace," he said turning to her, "would you mind calling the Adjutant General and tell him you are acting under my authority. I want all reservists activated immediately. Tell him I will be convening a conference call with him later this afternoon, but I want all of the Texas military ready for whatever happens in the aftermath."

"Yes," Grace said, "I will do that."

"Thank you, I want to do some prep in these final few minutes before we talk to the President," he said before taking the papers Ray had prepared and moving to his desk.

85.

Dante looked around at the sparse furnishings in Preston's apartment. It was similar enough to the hotel room he had spent the night in to make him dislike it. Although Dante considered himself a true socialist, he liked being at the top of the socialist hierarchy. He enjoyed the finer things in life, and felt that he deserved them because of the status he had acquired. He justified this belief by pointing out that even in the countries that had come closest to communism like China, Cuba, and the former Soviet Union, the leadership did not live the same way the masses did. It was clear by his manner of living that Preston thought differently, he might actually *be* a true believer.

"Dante," Preston smiled broadly while pouring him a cup of coffee," what an honor to have you here."

"It is my pleasure," Dante said, smiling back. He enjoyed being around someone like Preston, a sycophant that never made him feel compelled to express gratitude for being served. Dante almost forgot how much of a favor Preston was doing for him, almost believed that Preston *owed* him this service.

"Let me start by saying that you are a hero here, Dante," Preston glowed. "We are officially denying you had anything to do with the attacks in Texas of course, but amongst our followers, we are soooooo proud of you!"

Dante smiled uncomfortably as he anticipated for a moment that Preston was going to try to hug him. Thankfully, the Governor-elect maintained his distance. "Well, it was a good first step in the cause, wasn't it?" Dante said, moving slightly away from the hovering man before motioning for him to have a seat.

"I have some disappointing news," Preston said, sitting on a chair across from Dante. "Two of our scientists, the ones working on The Project," Preston said, making air quotes in an overly exaggerated manner, "have disappeared."

Dante looked up at him. "When?"

"Not sure," Preston said frowning, "they may have gotten cold feet after all of the excitement in California and Texas."

"Preston, do you have a security detail?" Dante asked.

"No," Preston smiled and waved his hands, "the people love me. I have no need for men with guns around me."

"You might want to reconsider that," Dante said as he rose and peered out onto the street from the window in Preston's apartment. Moving the curtain back into place when he was done.

"Why do you say that?" Preston asked. "I just won the election in a landslide, I have nothing to fear here."

Dante looked at him with pity. A true believer he was, but a mental giant he was not. This is what happens when people elect a young ideologue with no life experience or political sense he thought to himself. "Preston, not everyone is happy with your election, you do understand that, right?"

"What do you mean, Dante?" Preston looked hurt.

"I just mean that there are sometimes bad people out there that would look to do you harm is all," Dante said, in as much of a consoling voice as he could muster.

"Oh, the crazies you mean?" Preston waved off the idea as silly.

"They aren't all crazy, Preston," Dante said.

"After 'The Project' there will be less of them to worry about," Preston said with an eager smile. "Some of them will switch to our side, but all of them will be afraid to oppose us."

"That may be, and I hope you are right," Dante nodded. "But in the meantime, are you able to get us a security team? Didn't you mention on the phone that you had a safe place that no one could find?"

Preston smiles and opened his arms wide, "This is that place, Dante! You are safe here."

Down the block, in a dark blue minivan, a DPS agent downloaded the recording of the conversation, transferred it to an encrypted file, and sent it to Clark.

86.

"Mr. President, thank you for giving us an audience here today," Tim said as the video connection was established and the President of the United States appeared before them form his desk in the Oval Office. "I have with me my team," he continued and introduced Clark, Grace, Jack, and Ray.

"Good to see you, Governor," the President said with a big smile. President Dennis Logan was a pragmatic businessman, not overly idealistic but conservative enough on the right issues to drive the Left into a complete an utter outrage with every decision he made. Even on issues where he agreed with their long held idealistic beliefs, they argued with him and cast his intentions as impure or suspect even when his actions were those they claimed to want. As an outsider to politics, he had not bothered to "kiss the ring" of the Republican establishment either. As a result, he was not liked by either political party, but adored by the base of the Republican Party and by an overwhelming majority of the independent class of mostly apolitical voters. It was a strange coalition, but an effective one.

"Governor," the President began, "I have read your report on the events that preceded the attack on California, and I concur with your assessment that Dante Malone should be held accountable for the crimes he committed." The President spoke methodically, attentively. "I am also going to issue a public pardon to you and your team for any crimes that may have been committed in the killing of those special agents and the television crews."

Grace shifted in her seat, almost an imperceptible movement, but one that Ray noticed.

"However," President Logan continued sternly, "this needs to stop. Right here, and right now."

"Mr. President," Tim replied, "I would point out to you that there is still an ongoing threat in New York."

"You need to let this play out, Governor," President Logan continued. "And I mean, just let it go."

"Sir," Tim said, "if you are telling us to stand down because the federal government is going to take over this situation and bring both Dante Malone and the Governor-elect of New York to justice, then we will gladly to do so."

"Look, Tim, I don't want this to escalate," the President lowered his voice and began using his hands to talk now. His Northeastern accent was accentuated by the less formal dialogue he was shifting into. "In order to prevent that, I think we need to just call this even and move on."

Tim felt his heart begin to race, he was mindful to control his temper because of who he was talking to. "Sir, with all due respect, this is not even," he began. "We will bring them to justice if the federal government does not. If we do, the chances of a war between Texas, California, and New York are likely."

The President frowned and leaned back in his chair. "Why do you say it is likely?"

"I say it is likely because will not wait for it to start, we will strike first this time," Tim said looking directly at the President through the screen.

"I offer you a pardon and this is your response?" Logan said indignantly.

"I appreciate the thought behind that, sir, I do," Tim said respectfully. "But I don't think a pardon will mean a thing to me or my team if we cannot protect the people of Texas. Waiting this out, or letting it go as you suggest means simply waiting to be attacked again. I can't let that happen."

"So what are you saying, Governor?" the President asked, leaning forward and folding his hands together on his desk.

"Sir, I am asking you to take care of this, immediately," Tim paused. "If not, then I am telling you we will handle it ourselves." Tim sat looking at the screen, he would not plead with the President for help, but he was trying to be as respectful as possible.

"Well, you already have my answer," the President said with a shrug. "I said I think you should let it go, but you do what you feel you need to do, Tim. Let me know if I can help." The President motioned to disconnect the video feed and the screen went blank.

Tim leaned back in his chair and rubbed his eyes. "Ok, that went about as badly as it could possibly go," he said to his team.

"Well, not quite," Grace said, "at least he didn't threaten to arrest all of us."

"What does he mean, 'do what you feel you need to do?'" Clark asked. "Is he giving us encouragement or is he warning us? I couldn't tell."

"I think," Ray said, tapping his finger on the table lightly, "maybe he is ok with us taking action. I couldn't read him completely. I didn't get the sense that he was threatening us, but I also didn't get the idea that he wanted to encourage us either."

"I agree," Jack said. "It seems like he really just wants this to go away or solve itself in whatever way that happens."

"There is the possibility that he would be completely ok with a war," Grace said. Everyone turned to look at her and she continued. "I don't mean that he wants one, just that he might not think it would be the worst thing to happen if the country were to break into more idealistically homogenous pieces."

Tim scratched his chin. "So, you are saying he would not oppose a secession of some sort?"

"That's exactly what I am saying," Grace said. "Only he knows for certain, but maybe he is ok with that. Alternatively, maybe he thinks that fighting it out will *save* the country from dissolving into a bunch of sovereign nation states."

"Grace makes a good point," Ray said. "The President is not bashful about his reputation as a streetfighter. Every boy learns growing up that sometimes you have to fight, even with your friends, to straighten things out."

Jack nodded, "Very true. Maybe that is actually what he is thinking about all of this. Let the boys fight it out and they can be friends again later."

"Probably a bad time to point this out," Grace smiled, "but girls don't do that. Despite that, I agree with that as a possible consideration for this President."

"It is ironic that his election had us forgetting about all of the secession talk and now he might preside over it actually happening," Tim said. "Ok, but all of that is farther down the road. At hand, we have a decision to make."

Clark looked at him and said, "Sir, I think we have a consensus, but the final decision is yours."

"I understand, but if we do this," Tim paused, "if we do this there is the real possibility that we are starting a war. Are we all prepared to accept that as a realistic consequence of this decision, right here, right now? If we are reading the President wrong, if we attributing ideas to him that he does not hold, this could mean that we might be fighting our own government."

All of the heads in the room nodded solemnly.

"Sir, one correction to your statement," Grace said. "We didn't start this war. What we are all agreeing to here is finishing it."

Tim nodded. He stood up and slowly paced the room, stopping in front of the Texas and American flags standing side by side. He looked over at the flag on his wall with a cannon and a star above the phrase "Come and Take It." He moved slowly to the window and looked out over the District of Austin.

"Everything is changing," he said softly. "But Texas will always be Texas." He moved back to his seat and exhaled loudly before sitting down. "Clark, Jack, give the orders to execute the plan," he said. "May God help us."

86.

And thus began the War Between the States. The governor of California lay dead in an apartment in New York, where the Governor-elect of New York was kidnapped and taken to Texas to stand trial for conspiracy to commit murder. Initial speculation by the media of terrorism shifted to accusations of radical political ideologies, and finally to State identities. Within days, the ideological battle lines were formed and the remaining forty-seven states would began to pick sides.

The news media fell into ideological camps, becoming propaganda tools for their preferred states. For many in the media, this was less a development than an evolution that had begun long ago. Right and wrong were becoming relative in many circles, and Evangelical leaders pointed out that America was losing its moral compass. What was abundantly clear was that war was coming. It was churning, simmering, and occasionally breaking the surface, but the rolling boil was close at hand. New York and California vowed retaliation for the loss of their Governors. Texas continued its policy of not commenting on actions it may or may not have taken, but prepared quietly for a ground invasion of both states.

Whatever the outcome, the team that sat at the table that day and gave the order to start this off knew that Texas would defend herself, alone if necessary. Despite knowing the likely trajectory of such a decision, each left the table that day with the same prayer: "Long live the Republic, and God Bless America."

End: Book I

Author Bio

Luke Kent is a former police officer, police trainer, and policy analyst. He has worked with and trained hundreds of police officers in various capacities, and remains committed to the profession.